Beer, Women and Bad Decisions

by ·ris

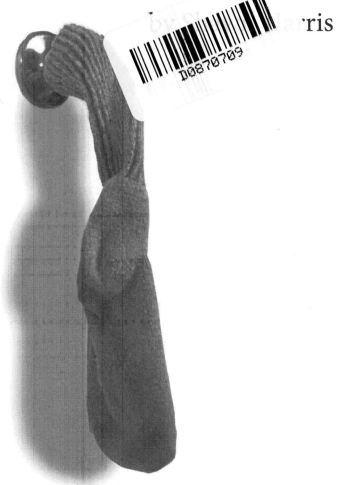

Illustrations by Jay Peteranetz
Visit us on the web at: www.ChooseTheEnding.com

Caution!

Intrepid Reader:

This book is unlike most as YOU will decide the result of this singular night on the town. From time to time, you will be given choices to make– decisions that will lead to fantasies fulfilled or to certain trouble, even death. When presented with a choice, take a moment to decide wisely. As I'm sure you know, your dick does not always make good choices for you.

Good luck reader… and wear a rubber.

What the hell am I doing with my life? you think as you stare into the bathroom mirror, clad in a wet towel after a satisfying shower.

It's been two months since Veronica left wearing only your oversized white shirt and some cute little panties with ducks on them.

"It's time for you to GROW UP!" she screamed as she clutched her pile of clothes, slamming the door shut. Honestly, you didn't see what the big deal was.

It was a Saturday. She was sleeping in. Having woken up earlier, you had been staring fondly at her for a few minutes. In the midst of appreciating her serene sleeping form, a mischievous grin broke across your face and you slowly pulled the covers over Veronica's head. *Whoooomp!* A muffled explosion akin to an oil refinery blowing up some ten miles away erupted under the covers. Dutch oven, baby!

With a startle, Veronica awoke, scratching at the covers attempting to gain an edge in order to pull them away and free herself from the smell.

"Goddammit! Let me out! Ugh! Oh Jesus! Let me out, asshole!"

You laughed and laughed as she struggled, finally freeing herself. With a look that could wither the most stalwart plant, Veronica climbed out of bed and proceeded to scoop up her belongings scattered around the floor from the night before.

"Come on, honey. I'm just messin' with ya. You're not honestly mad, are you?"

Looking up from her clothes scavenging efforts, Veronica glared venomously.

"Fuck. You." The deliberate enunciation of each word made it clear she was pissed.

And that was basically it. Out the door. No phone calls returned, no text messages answered. *Damn, she was pretty too.* You sigh.

You look back in the mirror at yourself. Twenty-eight years old, working full time at the Coffee Haus, some money in the bank but hardly using all the "potential" you were constantly told that you had growing up. You flex your biceps in the mirror. *Not horrible. Not amazing... but not horrible.*

You turn sideways and curl your arm, admiring your unfortunately average physique. You should go back to the gym and use that membership that seemed so promising when you bought it eight months ago. Maybe later this weekend. One more pose and your mind turns to tonight.

Tonight's gonna be the night! you tell yourself. *Time to get back on that horse and find someone new!* You walk over to your closet, fling open the doors and look at your clothing options.

Put on casual clothes.
Turn to page 4

Dress in a suit.
Turn to page 203

"And what bastard stole a horse?" Sofia looks at you confused.

_____

Uh-oh. Lie and go big!
Turn to page 313

The truth will set you free. 'Fess up.
Turn to page 133

"Sure dude, that'd be tight. Any pref on where to go?" you ask.

"Yeah totally. There's this new sports bar I heard about on the radio driving home. It's got all sorts of fuckin' huge-ass flat screens. I gotta think that place would be the bomb to catch the game tonight and throw down a few brews."

"Sounds good, I guess" you say with hesitation, thinking to yourself that watching the game is hardly the best way to meet a chick. But hey, maybe afterwards you guys can check out another place.

The two of you head out in Thad's car, shooting the shit about the Coffee Haus and the douchebags who complicate an order to the point where a simple cup of joe becomes a diatribe of ingredients, temperatures, and technique. *What fags.*

Sure enough, the sportsbar is everything that Thad described. Plenty of "huge-ass" LCD flat screen televisions broadcast sports throughout the bar. Best of all, one whole wall has a projection of the game which has just started. The enormous picture is probably as close to the real experience as you can get without shelling out fifty-five bucks for an actual ticket. The bar roars with the developing rowdy and raucous atmosphere. You and Thad score a small table on the floor facing the big screen.

The beer specials rock and it isn't long before you are cheering loudly at every good play and groaning equally so at every mistake. Pitcher after pitcher of cheap domestic beer arrives just in time so no glass reaches empty. As your buzz takes hold, you rapidly lose count of the number of pitchers the two of you consume. Your only expression as the game enters its final moments is a permanent shit-eating grin.

Oh Thank God, you think when a timeout is called. *Holy shit, I gotta pee!* No sooner thought then acted upon, you stand up and briefly sway before stumbling toward the pisser.

"Oh fuck, I'm totally sorry!" you blurt out as you uncontrollably list into a very attractive woman with long black hair. "I kinda drank an itty bitty bit too much" you smirk, showing the amount you drank between your fingers.

She smiles back, her eyes partly dimmed and red, the gaze of a fellow drinker.

"Fuggin' kick ass game, eh?" she says enthusiastically in a thick Jersey accent. With that, she departs into the women's bathroom, throwing the door open in a very unladylike way.

You take a piss that seems to go on for an eternity, passing the time by idly reading the stupid scrawl on the wall in front of you. Two taps and you're done.

Outside the restroom you pause for a second, wondering if you should wait for the chick you just met or if that would be weird. Before the decision makes it way through your alcohol-addled brain, the door opens to the women's bathroom and out comes the woman you bumped into.

"Hey… uh… like I think you're pretty cool." *Oh my God, what the hell is coming out of my mouth,* you think somewhere deep inside. "My buddy and I have a table over there and… like… it'd be cool to, you know, get to know each other better. Come over for a drink?"

The woman swings her head drunkenly around to look in the direction you're pointing. "Fuck it," she blurts out, "Sure. Why not. I'm Malissa." A hand juts out expecting a handshake which you haphazardly return.

The two of you stumble to your table and over the next couple of hours drink a staggering number of pitchers of beer, make small talk laced with swearing, and generally develop a mild drunkenly interest in each other. Finally, Malissa leans over and asks what time it is.

You look at your watch. It's 10:29 p.m.

"Oh Jeeesus," she slurs, "I gotta go. And I gotta pee. Ok. I'm going to pee, then I'm going to go. I'll be right back."

Malissa lurches wildly back to the bathroom, steadying herself with unsuspecting bar patrons along the way, managing to knock over only one empty pitcher. After a few minutes and a difficult journey back, Malissa plops herself down in her chair.

"Ok, I'm gonna go. You're cute," she says as she drunkenly reaches out to touch your face, deciding halfway there to give it a playful slap instead. "Whatcha say we go get some coffee?" Her eyes meander over to Thad. "Sorry roomie, there's only room for <u>him</u>." She points in your direction. "Tough titties, kitty." She giggles at her own joke and stands up wavering beside the table like a sapling in a windstorm.

Thad looks at you. You obviously have a decision to make: stay with Thad and see if something better comes along or check out early with the chick from Jersey.

Bros before Hos, man! Besides, there are tons of other beautiful drunk woman here to meet, greet and eat.
Turn to page 11

Sorry dude, I'm out. I'm takin' this chance and gunna bounce with Malissa.
Turn to page 20

You swallow hard and steal yourself for the expedition to come. (You inwardly smile, proud of your double entendre.)

You stand up and strip down, taking her on the orange shag rug. After ten embarrassing minutes as a muff miner without a headlamp, victory is had. The groans of your lovemaking intermix with those of her roommate's and the pounding bass of Soul Train blaring in the background. You feel like John Holmes.

After a gushing climax– Foxy reaching to the heavens while straddling your mighty cock– she collapses on top of you, panting. The two of you lay there for a few minutes, enjoying the ripples of energy pulsing through your nerves. Eventually, Foxy pulls herself off your waist and reaches across to fumble in her purse on the chair. With a satisfactory "Ah-hah!" she withdraws her near empty pack of Virginia Slims. She pulls two out, puts them both in her mouth, lights them and hands one to you. You take the slim cigarette and inhale a long, deep pull– the smoke burns your throat and lungs. You close your eyes and let yourself slip back into the moment.

The next morning, you wake to an empty bed and the sound of breakfast cooking. Having left your clothes in the living room the night before, you find a robe of Foxy's that will fit, and make your way to the kitchen. Laverne and Schneider are already awake, talking at the space-age white table. Foxy brings over breakfast and the four of you sit down to a scrumptious feast of Shit on a Shingle.

A few days later, you notice something peculiar that gets you worried. Every time you pee, it kinda burns. You try drinking more water in case your urine is just too concentrated, but it doesn't help. Soon thereafter you also develop a fever. Worried, you head to see a doctor who informs you that you have the worst case of Chlamydia he's seen since 1978. You just smile– Foxy's left you a souvenir from a decade long past.

The End

You look up at Malissa, smile, and tell her *sorry*. It's not even eleven p.m. and you can't leave Thad hangin' like that. Dude's your homie, after all! She rolls her eyes in response.

"Ok. Whatever. Adios muchachos." With a drunken flourish Malissa leaves, this time knocking over a chair and bumping into another patron so hard he spills his beer down the front of his shirt.

You and Thad order another pitcher of beer and toast your glasses to solidarity.

"Fuck that bitch, dude. There was no WAY I was gonna tap that skank. She totally wasn't worth it." you tell Thad and yourself.

"Yeah dude, like her accent and all... I could barely understand that chick!"

"Totally dude. Besides, look at all these other chickas. This night is just getting started, motherfucker!" you say with conviction.

Unfortunately, between the ridiculous number of beers and your pitiful drunken attempts at hitting on the "bitches", the night never does "get started" and at two a.m., you and Thad are kicked out.

"Whatcha wanna do, bro?" Thad asks as the two of you are standing outside the door, swaying back and forth like goldfish in a bag held by an excited two year old. "Wanna walk home or cab it? I'm down-diggity-down with either."

You jam you hand in your pocket and with difficulty (*Goddamn...pocket!*), pull out your wallet. You have enough to get you closer to your house but not enough to get you all the way home, and Thad is broke. *Dammit! When did beer get so friggin' expensive?*

Take the cab part way?
Turn to page 12

Go ahead and just hoof it.
Turn to page 13

You phone a taxi and about twenty minutes later, one shows up. The two of you stumble in through the same door. You tell the driver you only have eight dollars so take you as far as you can get toward home.

After $6.48 racks up on the meter, the driver pulls over. "This is it, boys. This is as far as I go.

"But there's not eight bucks on the meter!" you protest.

"The hell I'm gonna drive out to bumblefuck and not get a tip. This is it. End of the line."

You'd like to retort with some great argument of how this is highway robbery and how he is completely taking advantage of you in your drunkenly state, but instead you just angrily hand him the money, words failing you completely.

You and Thad hoof it the rest of the way back home and your "big night out" ends with you passed out drunk on the couch, hands down your pants, QVC blaring away about the latest and greatest hand cream.

The End

"Screw it man. Let's just walk" you say. "It's not all that far and God knows, I could use the time to sober up a little."

The streets are deserted– the night air silent save for the two of you drunkenly babbling. You and Thad take off toward home, weaving back and forth, sometimes missing each other, other times colliding. You talk about the game and the chicks you didn't hit on but should've and would've if the bar hadn't closed so damn early.

"Dude, that blonde was totally looking at you, bro. She WANTED you. I could totally tell," Thad says. You burst out laughing.

"Shit dude, I didn't want that raggamuffin. She was all you."

After a few blocks, you put your arm around Thad's shoulders.

"Helluva night dude." you say, louder than necessary– the alcohol having long removed any sense of volume control you had. You glance at your watch under the neon lights of a tattoo parlor while riding the great ship Sidewalk home.

"Shhhhit. It's three a.m."

"Dude!" Thad suddenly blurts out. "Check it out! Let's get a tattoo! Fuckin' A, that's a great idea. We TOTALLY need tattoos. Chicks go apeshit over 'em!"

Hell yeah! Let's get tattoos!
Turn to page 14

That's a bad idea.
Turn to page 18

"Definitely!" you say, any other thoughts of reason cast aside by the alcohol flowing freely through your veins.

The two of you walk inside. The pink neon light through the window illuminates the counter and mixes harshly with the dim fluorescents overhead. A lone figure sits behind the counter, smoking a cigarette. A long stem of ash barely holds on. He looks at the two of you briefly then goes back to reading the paperback in his hands. You stagger up to a large three ring binder on the counter and start thumbing through the pages, seeing possible tattoos you could request.

"I'm totally getting barbed wire around my bicep!" Thad exclaims. "Chicks dig a dude with wire. They totally think it makes you look dangerous."

You keep thumbing through the images until you settle upon an Aztec symbol that looks balls.

"Guys know what you want?" the heavily tattooed man asks nonchalantly, moving the cigarette to an overflowing ashtray.

"Yeah, I'm going wire dude, fully thugged out." Thad exclaims.

"Fine. Sit over there," he says brusquely and points to a ratty articulated chair in the corner.

Thad staggers over and plops down drunkenly in the seat. A bank of needles sits ominously nearby. He pulls up his sleeve and soon thereafter high pitched buzzing fills the room. After a stint of watching, you grow bored and start meandering around the shop.

You notice another chair nearby for people to get tattoos in more risqué places and make your way over to it. *I'm just going to sit here for a second,* you think, lying back on the reclined chair. *It's all good.* You close your eyes.

When you come too, you're home in the living room. Groggily you stand up, your head pounding, your lower back sore from sleeping on the worn-out couch. You wonder how you got home, but whatever. You grab a tall glass of water from the kitchen, four ibuprofen and make your way to the bathroom for a hot shower.

In one go, you drink the entire glass of water, disrobe, and jump in the shower. Hot water spills over you, washing away the sin of the night before.

After standing in the shower until fully pruned under lukewarm water, you finally get out. You towel yourself off and notice that your lower back is still tender. It's sore but superficially so– different than it usually is from sleeping on the couch. With your hand, you wipe away the steam on the mirror and turn around to take a look at your back.

There, right above your asscrack, is a trampstamp of a pegasus/unicorn hybrid flying over a rainbow.

"Thad!"

The End

"Pshaw! You're WAY drunker than I am," you respond. "Remember, I was only drinking beer for most of the night."

She rolls her eyes. "Fine, whatever. Let's go."

The two of you go out to the parking lot. You unlock her door first as a show of chivalry. She doesn't even really seem to notice. Once inside, you turn to her and ask for the address of the club she wants to hit.

"I don't really remember," she tells you. "Let's just head downtown near the library and I'll recognize it when we get close."

You back out of the parking lot and squeal your tires as you take off toward the city. *Time to show this chick a little about driving.* You push down the accelerator and zoom toward the darkened city buildings ahead. Cars pass by as if they were standing still as you deftly leave them quickly behind.

"I don't think we're going to make the light," Kera warns you as you plow toward an intersection with a yellow light.

"Fuck that baby, I got it. Don't worry about it." You drop the car down a gear and push the accelerator to the floor.

The light ahead of you turns red and two opposing cars on the cross street come at each other, passing next to one another in the intersection ahead. You slam on your brakes, but it's too late. You haven't bought new tires in years and your current bald tires have little gripping power left. You slam into the front side of the first car.

The defective airbag in your steering wheel fails to deploy. With all your horny haste to get to the next club, you never buckled up either. Your head slams into the windshield and you knock yourself cold.

A few hours later, you awaken strapped to a bed in the ER, stark fluorescent lights shine overhead. You blink your eyes rapidly trying to acclimate to the blinding light. A nurse passes by and you fire off a million questions at her all at once.

"What's going on? Where am I? How's Kera? Why the hell am I strapped down on this fuckin' uncomfortable bed?"

"Whoa. Whoa. Whoa. Settle down. Calm yourself, sir," the nurse says as she walks over. You struggle against your restraints pathetically as the pain caused by it is a great deterrent. The nurse removes a syringe from a nearby drawer, fills it from a cracked ampoule, and injects it into your IV. Within seconds your struggling stops and you ease into a comfortable demeanor, the drugs taking over.

"Sir, I have some bad news for you. The car accident you were in was a pretty bad one. You have multiple lacerations from the windshield and you've done severe damage to your spinal cord. The woman you were traveling with was not wearing her safety belt, and it doesn't look good for her."

Many months and three surgeries later, you sit in your wheelchair facing a computer, a joystick in your hand, playing solitaire. It's been an uphill battle to even get to this point. You pause moving your four of clubs to reflect once again on what happened during that horrible accident– the accident that did this to you and killed that chick Kera. You close your eyes, trying in vain to remember her face.

A strong salty odor with overtones of ammonia greets your nostrils. You open your eyes and look down. Yup, your catheter bag is leaking again.

The End

The two of you stand outside the bar, bathed in the soft light filtering out through the front window between painted ads of beer specials. Both of you sway unconsciously as you stand there, bumping into each other with the rhythm of the imaginary ocean below your feet. Within five minutes a large Lincoln Town Car pulls up– gleaming wire wheels slow to a stop. The driver's door opens and out steps a large man in a dark gray suit, a thick mop of hair on his head and one third of a cigar in his mouth.

"Evenin' Ms. Taladuchi. See ya been havin' a goot time. And who's this schmuck you'd wit?" the driver says, his voice thick with a Brooklyn accent.

"Eh Carlos, you be nice, k? He's a good guy." Malissa responds, her accent growing thicker in present company.

The driver merely grunts and opens the door for her. "Geddin."

Inside the car are finely oiled leather seats and the smell of cigars mixed with aged scotch. The seats are immaculate as if you were the first passengers since the car rolled off the assembly line in 1987. As the car revs up and pulls out, Malissa is all over you, kissing your neck, reaching down your pants. You want to be turned on, but the alcohol coupled with an audience from the driver makes it difficult. After two minutes of Malissa's love attack, a booming voice comes bouncing off the windshield toward the backseat.

"Heys there loveboids! Don't be go fuggin' up my leathah back dere. I ain't gonna be wipin' out no goddamn shit from your monkey love, got it?"

Malissa just snickers and sits back, her hand still resting down your pants. You look at his angry eyes in the rear view mirror and have a hinting suspicion that you've seen his face somewhere before. The Sopranos? Maybe the movie "Casino"? Either way, he doesn't seem all that friendly.

After a short drive you stop in front of a stylish townhome.

"I thought we were going to get coffee?" you ask.

"Oh yeah. Dammit. So, uh, you wanna come in? I can make some for ya."

"I don't think dat's a good idea Ms. Taladuchi, what with bein' snockered an all. Ya father wouldn't like et very much," answers Carlos for you.

"Lissen here, Carlos. You wouldn't tell, wud ya? I mean, he's a nice fella. Look at 'im."

"Listen dearie, I ain't takin' no shit from Mr. Taladuchi on yous account. No guests, not tonight."

Malissa looks at you, pouting girlishly. "I'm sorry. Here lemme give ya my digits and yous can cawl me tomorrah, k?" After some furiously concentrated digging, she grabs a receipt and pen from her clutch. In a barely discernable shaky scrawl reminiscent of a first grader, she writes her phone number on the receipt.

Malissa hands you the paper, exits the car and turns to blow you a kiss. She then stumbles up to her front door, almost faceplanting when her foot catches a small step on the path. You close the car door and look anxiously at the driver.

"Hey… uh… Mr. Carlos, sir? Think you could give me a ride home? I only live like twenty minutes from here."

"Hmmmm…I guess I's could do dat for ya." Carlos begrudgingly responds.

The two of you drive in silence back to the main road. When prompted, you give Carlos rough directions to your place. However, after ten minutes or so, Carlos takes an unexpected left onto the interstate.

You are about to protest when Carlos speaks up, "Hey, I gotta littl' errand to run. Yous don't mind, do ya?"

You look at your watch. It's quarter past eleven and while the time doesn't bother you, being with Carlos any longer than necessary doesn't seem like a good idea. On the other hand, disagreeing with him also doesn't seem like a good idea.

Finally Carlos pounds his fist on the bar screaming, "Non rompermi il cazzo!" With a fluid sweep, he brushes open his coat to reveal a shoulder holster carrying his gun. You can't take your eyes off what is happening. Every fiber of your being tells you to run, duck, do SOMETHING, but no part of you moves.

With a reach across his chest, Carlos goes for his gun. Unfortunately he never has time to withdraw it as a huge explosion erupts from the bar in front of him, shattering the woodwork, leaving a huge hole in the paneling and his waist.

"HOLY FUCKING SHIT!" you scream as the shotgun blast wakes you forcefully from your spectator nature and shocks you into the reality of the situation.

The barkeep turns his eyes toward you and starts to unfasten the straps holding the shotgun in place under the bar. You cast around looking for an exit.

Do you run for the door to the street?
Turn to page 26

Do you run for the kitchen entrance?
Turn to page 28

You fall back off the bar chair, instantly sober and cast about frantically for the shortest path out to the street and hopeful salvation. You run, flinging chairs aside and dodging tables as you plow full speed for the front door.

"Vai a fare in culo! Me ne frego dei suoi ordini!"

You keep running, ignoring whatever the barkeep is saying. It's not important. You've never really faced death before and the fear is overpowering. Adrenaline courses through you, giving you speed and endurance– a few more yards to freedom.

BOOM! It sounds like a cannon going off in the room and you feel buckshot ripping through your back. The blast throws you to the floor.

You hear footsteps pounding on the well worn floor, sole smacking wood, coming to finish you off. You start crawling toward the door, every motion rips the tears in your back further. Your face is hot and your vision blurry from tears of dread. Before you can make it even a few feet, a searing pain rips through your side as the barkeep kicks you onto your back. He levels the gun at your head. Instinctively, you throw up your hands in surrender, your eyes blinking uncontrollably, unable to stare down the dark throat of the weapon that will soon end your pathetic life.

"I'm not with him! I swear to fucking God! I'm not with that mother fucker! Oh God Virgin Mary, I'm not with him. You have to believe me! I just met him. He dragged me here! Oh God Oh God Oh God!"

"Non raccontar frenge!" the barkeep screams back at you.

"I fucking swear it, oh God, I fucking swear it. I never met that asshole till tonight when I got a fucking ride with Malissa."

The barkeep looks hard at you and slowly the gun descends to his side. When you realize there's a chance you may live after all, you begin to weep uncontrollably with relief, blubbering "Thank you" over and over again.

The barkeep angrily points to the door in front of you. "Vai in mona!" evidently telling you to get the fuck out.

Despite the intense pain, you get to your feet and manage to stumble out of the Italian eatery. Once outside, you painfully pull out your phone and call for an ambulance before you pass out from exhaustion and pain.

Some time later, you wake up in the ER. The clock on the wall says it's after ten in the morning. You take in a difficult breath, the wounds in your back straining against the air filling your lungs. You let it out in a big sigh. You're alive.

The End

You push back forcefully from the bar. Your chair catches on the rug underneath sending you toppling hard onto your back. You roll over and scramble to rise, making your way quickly toward the double stainless steel doors leading to the kitchen.

"Pisciasotto!" you hear the barkeep scream after you.

Inside the kitchen you find yourself surrounded by an ocean of stainless steel. Every surface glistens in the bright fluorescent light overhead. You know you don't have long until the barkeep gets his shotgun unhooked and comes hunting for you.

In an act of self-preservation, you drop to the floor, hoping that by keeping low you won't cause nearly the reflection you would otherwise in this house of mirrors.

On your hands and knees, you start crawling frantically around the kitchen floor; the spongy black mats protect your knees from the tile underneath. *It's like a fucking maze in here!* you think to yourself. *There has to be a door somewhere for deliveries or something.* You continue to crawl until you hear the door to the dining room swing open and the distinct cock of a shotgun reloading.

The sound causes you to freeze instantly. You turn your head to look around but on all fours, your range of vision is somewhat limited. You quietly continue forward at a snail's pace to the end of the counter and sit there, knees to your chest, assessing your options.

Ok, pissed off Italian with shotgun. Check. Lost in shiniest kitchen ever. Check. Totally fucked. Check.

You look guardedly around at your surroundings. There are some baking sheets immediately in front of you and a stack of frying pans to your right.

Try to hatch a plan with the baking sheets?
Turn to page 53

Think the frying pans make a better asset?
Turn to page 41

Mosey down to The ShitKicker.
Turn to page 35

Ease on down to Blaxploitation.
Turn to page 164

"Seriously Thad, as much fun as Blaxploitation sounds, I think I'd rather hit the other bar." Frankly, you feel more than a little worried about your disco skills.

"That's cool. No worries, bud. I'm ready to ride the bull tonight, so let's go!" Thad exclaims in a pseudo-Texan accent. On your way out you snatch a dark cowboy hat from the closet.

The two of you catch a taxi downtown as the sun starts to fade over the horizon to the west.

As the taxi arrives at your destination, you think you recognize this place as somewhere you've been before. You are about to say something when Thad voices the same question.

"Didn't this place used to be 'Bulls and Babes'?"

"That's what I thought too!" you respond. Bulls and Babes was killer, so here's hoping that The ShitKicker has taken it up a notch. You exit the cab and stand in front of the enormous building. Overhead a neon pair of cowboy boots with slowly revolving spurs brightly illuminates the parking lot. Assessing the entering crowd, you're positive that being dressed to kill in a place where most are dressed to shovel shit is going to be the formula for riding some untamed country pussy later.

You enter the joint. The place is laid out like a roller skating rink from back in the day. There is a massive elliptical dance floor surrounded by chest-high tables spread out over a floor littered with peanut shells and sawdust. Your roomie grabs a couple of domestics from the bar as you score a table close to the dance floor.

Over the next hour, the two of you play "fuck or flee" with the dancing women. Many of them fall in the former category, looking very promiscuous in their skin-tight, country-themed outfits.

One lady in particular stands out to you with her large, blonde hair expertly styled around strong facial features. Her low cut dress barely hides a generous chest. She's a real Barbie doll.

"Dude, she's the one," you say as you elbow your roommate and point her out.

"I dunno," he replies doubtful. "See that big, burly guy next to her? I think they're together. They've been dancing every fuckin' song for the past hour."

"Fuck that. I don't see it. Dude has been next to her, yes, but he hasn't made a move, so I say she's fair game. Watch and learn my friend."

Confidently, you stand up and make your way to the dance floor. Within a few claps and a shimmy kick, you're dancing next to the bombshell you've singled out. A few more minutes and the song ends... now's your chance.

Offer to buy her a drink?
Turn to page 38

Pat her on the ass and tell her you like her dancing?
Turn to page 37

In a forthcoming manner, you pull back and slap "Barbie" playfully on her ass as you say, "Nice footwork there, honey!"

The blonde turns toward you, a half-smile crossing her face. You smile back not noticing the right hook coming quickly toward your chin. CRACK! You fall to the floor, consciousness fading. As the tunnel vision closes in, you see the blonde lean in close and whisper in a hoarse, deep voice. "Don't get fresh with me, motherfucker." You pass out.

The End

You turn your attention back to the surrounding curtain and continue your circumference of the club.

While you deal with the curtain, you are constantly being jostled by those dancing. One guy, wearing ridiculous yellow kitchen gloves actually grabs your arm as you pass by, leaning in close with a loose smile, glazed eyes settling on your own. You rip your arm away from his gloved hand, telling him to go fuck himself and continue on.

After a few moments, you start feeling weird. You can't seem to keep your thoughts straight. Your head starts spinning and the dancers around you begin to blur. You look down at your arm where that jackass grabbed you and notice a tab of paper sticking to your wet skin. *Holy shit, I've been dosed,* you realize.

The crowd around mutates as their individual edges exaggerate. Before you know it, you find yourself surrounded by huge cartoon characters. They all laugh at you as you stand under a single raincloud in a huge green meadow. You begin to cry because everyone is being so mean and hurtful! Your only refuge is to hunker down next to the curtained wall. The curtain morphs into a great window shade, and you want nothing more than to pull it down between yourself and all those laughing cartoon bastards.

Forty-five minutes later, you are found by the fire department huddled between the curtain and the wall, bawling your eyes out, complaining about ruthless bunnies and wolves that won't stop mocking you. It takes five of them to cajole you from hiding.

Wet and confused, you wander the streets in a haze until morning, looking for wild daffodils and magical sunflowers to brighten your cartoon day.

The End

"You know, I'd love to see the stacks; but honestly, my stomach is still a little unsettled from tonight's activities and I'd hate to yack all over the volumes of history you have stored down there. Another time?"

"Oh. Ok. That's a good idea."

"How about we head to my place instead and we'll keep the 'party' going there?" you say with an edge of jest to your voice. "I'll put on a fresh pot of coffee and we'll watch the sun rise from my roof," you suggest.

Sam agrees and follows you back to your place in her car. After another cup of coffee and Sam's confession of her love for 18th century Spanish literature, the two of you climb up to your roof. You sit close together on the blanket you brought up, backs against the chimney.

Silently, you and Sam watch the sun gently break the horizon, splaying out its welcoming rays, lighting up the tall billowing clouds overhead. It's a very cool moment that you share in mutual silence. As the sun illuminates the myriad neighborhoods sprawled out before you, you turn and look at Sam who's still fixated on the sun's climb into the sky. You gently reach up and turn her head toward you. She smiles. Slowly, as the light around you waxes, you lean in and kiss her gently on her welcoming lips.

The two of you climb back down and have a lovely morning of making love until exhausted, finally falling asleep. When you awake, you hear the sounds of eggs frying downstairs and the pop of the toaster delivering its golden product. You place your hands behind your head and look up at the ceiling. You sigh deeply and roll on your side, seeing a large tome of War and Peace sitting on the pillow next to you. You smile.

The End

"Hell yeah, I'd love to see the library and all the old books." A partial lie. What you REALLY want is to bone her in the stacks. "I'm guessing you have a key?"

"Yeah, of course. Let's go. And since it looks like you're still a little drunk, how about I drive? My Fiat's parked out front."

"Okey dokey, smokie. Sounds good to me."

You pay and head outside to Sam's beaten up, forest green Fiat. The doors squeak in protest when you get in. The ride's a bit bumpy, which doesn't help your developing headache, but the library is relatively close so it's not unbearable. The two of you park behind the massive granite structure and enter in through a steel door unlocked via Sam's keycard.

Inside, dim light illuminates beautiful marble floors sprouting rotund columns. You feel as if you are wandering through a petrified forest of finely honed trunks. You find it hard to talk above a reverent whisper.

"So where's the door to the archive?" you ask in a low voice.

"What?" Sam asks back loudly, her voice resonating off the hard surrounding surfaces.

"Sorry. I guess I'm just accustomed to whispering in libraries. My bad. So, where's the archive?" you ask again at a normal volume.

"It's three floors down from here. We'll have to use the freight elevator since the passenger one doesn't go there. It's just around the corner."

The freight elevator is a huge industrial number with horizontal doors that open in stages– first an outer set of metal doors followed by an interior set of steel mesh screens. The walls of the elevator are lined with quilted moving blankets, lending an air of a giant mobile padded cell for transporting crazy people. The two of you board amid a huge amount of clamor from the doors opening and closing. Slowly the elevator descends to archives below.

"So how many books are stored down here?" you ask trying to make conversation during the slow ride.

"Oh God, I don't know for sure. I know it's several hundred thousand at least. Some of the volumes go back to the early 1800's although they are stored in a climate controlled area I don't have access to– old bastard gatekeeper biddies. I guess I'm just 'too young' to handle the books, so I'm not given a key. God, it's like you have to have been born two centuries ago to handle the fucking books. Argh!" Sam espouses with clenched fists before catching herself. "Sorry, I just get all riled up about it."

The elevator clunks with a resonant **THUD** and the outer doors part. Sam opens the interior mesh doors and exits the elevator. You step out after her; although rather than closing the doors, she goes back into the elevator and pulls down one of the quilts from the wall.

"Never know when you might need something like this." Sam smiles slyly at you and you can feel yourself getting hard. *Hell yeah. We're gonna have sex in a library! How fucking cool is that?!* You shift yourself so that nothing is too apparent. *Don't want to jinx it.* Sam folds the quilt and hands it to you. You promptly hold it low near your waist to conceal "the General" and follow her into the darkened world beyond the elevator's dimly lit foyer.

"Hmmm... ah, here it is." Sam says after a few minutes of walking. She flips a couple switches and dim fluorescent light bathes the voluminous number of texts around you. You look around. There are books everywhere the eye can see, an infinite universe of texts. Sam takes your free hand and leads you into the depths of the archive.

"Here. I want to show you some wicked cool ancient maps I found the other week. It's a bit of a trek, but I think I remember how to get there."

Sam leads you through the labyrinth of books, turning right then left then a myriad of other turns– so many so that you quickly become disoriented. Every time you cross into a new aisle, you cast a glance this way and that looking for at least a wall to gauge your relative position on the floor, but none appear.

"Holy shit, this place is gigantic! How the hell do you ever find anything down here?"

Sam laughs. "Oh lemme tell ya, my first week of work, I got lost down here for six hours. Only by shouting for help for the last hour did I finally get someone to help me escape. At this point though, I feel like the minotaur on Crete navigating these twists and turns without a second thought."

"Righteous," you reply simply. All around you ragged spines of long past published works pass by in a blur of brown and black leather, the gilded lettering of their titles providing the merest highlight in an otherwise dingy environment devoid of real color.

After an eternity of walking with a hard-on and dirty thoughts clouding your mind, you finally stop. Sam takes the quilt from you. She lays it on the floor between the massive stacks and sits down on it. You gingerly sit down across from her, trying to hide how you feel in your pants, wondering where this amazing map collection must be. Sam looks at you through her stylish, black horn-rimmed glasses.

"You didn't honestly think I was going to show you maps, did you?"

"Uh. Well, I was kinda hoping not since I really am having a difficult time focusing right now."

"Oh, is it the remnant of booze or that mighty hard-on you've been so desperately concealing since we got off the elevator?" You blush a little but are happy that Sam's heading the way you were hoping she might. "How about you undress that handsome body of yours here and I'll undress in the aisle next door."

You're a bit surprised by her modesty, but fuck it. Whatever. Sam stands up and walks to the adjacent aisle. As you disrobe, you periodically catch glimpses of Sam pulling off her clothes between the rows of books. The effect is mesmerizing, almost dirty, as if you are at a shady peepshow. Many times you catch yourself pausing, transfixed by a glimmer of skin, the barest hint of a nipple or the graceful curvature of her back as it meets her ass.

A few minutes later, Sam comes around the corner– a beauty who captures your attention with an unrelentingly fervor. Her lithe, pale figure graced with full, round breasts and perky pink nipples stuns you. She is still wearing her black-rimmed glasses and her hair is still up in its bun, a foil of practicality to the nakedness below. Sam approaches you and the two of you engage passionately. You enter Sam almost immediately causing her to moan invitingly in response.

The two of you enjoy each other completely, alone amid treasures of the written word. During a moment of ecstasy while taking her from behind, Sam flagrantly knocks a row of books on the floor, her arms shooting out with abandon, screaming with pleasure. It's sex like you've never had before, dangerous and open, the feeling of nakedness in a public place. You finish on the quilt and it's everything you hoped and fantasized it would be. As you climax, the musty smell of the books mixed with the sweet lavender smell of her skin sets you on fire. You collapse afterwards, breathing heavily in the floral scent of her freed cascades of hair. The two of you embrace and within moments you are asleep.

When you awaken, you feel cold and the ground is scratchy. You rouse yourself and notice that you're lying on the industrial carpet that covers the floor of the archive. What's more, you're alone. Sam is gone, the quilt is gone and more importantly, your clothes are gone! *What the fuck is going on here?* You call out Sam's name, halting when you see the note propped up on the shelf next to you. You grab it to read it.

Had a great night. Thanks! --Sam

_____

Stay put. It's just a joke and she'll be back.
Turn to page 303

Try to find Sam.
Turn to page 30

Ok, baking sheets. What the hell can I do with baking sheets? you think. *Maybe wait until he gets close and whack him?* Stupid idea, you decide. *How about body armor?* You pause. That's not a half bad idea! With your baggy hoody, you could easily tuck one in front and one in back and anchor them by tucking them into your pants. You look at the thickness of the metal, trying to gauge if it's enough to stop buckshot. You shake your head slightly back and forth, unsure of the answer.

As quiet as you possibly can, you remove two baking sheets from the stack. You slide one under your hoody in front of your chest. It's awkward but it seems to offer at least some semblance of protection. With a bit more difficulty, you don a second pan to protect your back.

Alright. It's now or never. You stand up awkwardly, trying to keep the baking pans in place. You see the crazy Italian off to the left, partially hidden by an upper row of cabinets. A quick glance around and you find an exterior door, one aisle over.

You bolt for the exit, not attempting to muffle the clatter of your motion, putting your faith in your quickly hatched plan.

BOOM! An explosion of buckshot rips supersonically through the air, catching you in the back. The force of the blow slams you against the steel counter, your baking sheet in front distributing the impact. Unfortunately, your chin hits hard on the counter's edge as you fall to the floor.

SHIT! That HURT! Your back is wicked sore, but one hasty swipe tells you that you're not bleeding. *This armor shit works!*

You scramble to gain footing again, your sore back protesting against your aggressive move toward the exit.

Click-chunk. You hear the cock of the next round entering the chamber. A metallic ring sings out as the brass end of the spent cartridge bounces on the steel counter. Goddammit, you're close.

You reach out to grab the handle as you hear the blast of the shotgun again. Your legs fail you unceremoniously.

You crumple to the floor, your legs now piles of meat exposed through a ripped denim casing. The pain is blinding and it's hard to concentrate on anything.

The sound of the shotgun cocking again greats your ears followed by an unexpected click. The Italian lets loose a furious tirade and cocks the gun again. He pulls the trigger. Click. It's empty.

Despite the darkness closing in, you force yourself to focus entirely on getting out. You squirm closer to the door, pulling yourself hand over hand across the black floor mat. Excruciating pain shocks your body with each motion. You reach out, desperately trying to reach the knob which seems miles away.

You hear the clatter of the shotgun being thrown down on the steel counter and within seconds you feel a piercing pain rip through your outstretched shoulder. Your arm drops to the ground next to you, a clean slit through your hoody rapidly spilling out blood.

You've reached your limit and collapse into the blood pooling on the floor from your shoulder. Tears course down your face.

"Please don't kill me. Please. Please. I didn't do anything. I don't know that guy that you shot. He fuckin' kidnapped me. OH GOD, please. Please. Please don't kill me," you beg, face down, waiting for the inevitable.

Roughly, you are rolled over onto your back, sending a wave of pain screaming through your body. Through teary eyes and blurred vision, you look up at the Italian, his well pressed suit hardly muddled– a single red splatter decorates his crisp linen shirt cuff. You continue to beg, sending out spittle mixing with blood, crying uncontrollably.

Without a word, a fierce business-like focus on his face, he kneels and expertly slices open your throat, a skill gained through dressing meat daily for his chefs. The expensive knife cuts through the soft tissue of your throat with ease. You spill out across the floor.

The End

"You know, I would totally love to invite you along but I'm already gonna hook up with some friends. Another time?" you lie.

"Oh, ok." Thad looks a little crestfallen. He's like a puppy though, you can swat him with a newspaper and he'll be your best friend again in half an hour.

You take off, swinging the door shut behind you. At the curb, you reach into your hoody's front pocket and pull out a set of keys affixed to an old brass keyring and your trusty blue aluminum bottle opener.

With a quick jingle, you're in your 2002 Toyota Celica. The engine starts right up, *good ol' rice burners.* You turn on 101.5 and music fills the car punctuated occasionally by the tinny crackle of the speaker you blew in the back. You figure tonight's best bet is the It'll Do Lounge and Bar, a twenty minute drive from your house. It's not the nicest place, but it's got a mellow atmosphere and a frequently attractive crowd of singles.

Once there, you lock up the car and stroll in. The dark interior has relatively low ceilings and a well-worn, pitted wooden floor. You survey the scene with a keen eye– your gaze coming to rest on a bombshell at the far side of the bar. She's playing some video game sitting on top of the counter. You stride over, pull up a stool close (but not too close) and order a Brownstone Lager– full bodied, nice high alcohol content.

After a few minutes and a few drinks of your brew, you cast your eye over again at Ms. Rockin' Body. She's wearing a midnight blue dress with spaghetti straps, nicely low cut. The dress falls away from her slender body giving way to legs that go on forever sheathed in tall thigh-high black leather boots. *Holy shit,* you think to yourself. *That is one _fine_ ass piece of woman.*

She swears to herself. It's obvious her quarter ran out and she didn't do all that great. *Here we go!*

"Hey. Whatcha playing over there?" you ask coyly.

"It's one of those photo games. You have to figure out what six things are different between the two photos. It's great because they use these horrible 1980's porno pics. It's like finding an old issue of Penthouse from 1982 complete with big hair and Magnum PI cars. It's pretty sexcellent." She giggles at the absurdity of the whole thing.

"Sounds pretty sweet! Mind if I try?" you ask with feigned interest.

"Sure. Be my guest."

You slide your stool over to sit next to her and drop in a quarter. Sure enough, it's exactly as she said– a black woman with close-cropped bleached blonde hair poses with a large fluffy cat on her couch, her negligee falling seductive over her toned, dark body. The pastel Florida-themed décor of the room in the photo reminds you vividly of some castoff set from "Miami Vice". Super cheesy, not a great turn on. With help, you touch the six areas of the photo on the right that are photoshopped to be different from the photo on the left. You make it through three sets of photos before your time runs out and the game ends.

"Pretty bitchin, huh?!" the woman comments excitedly.

"It's something, alright" you respond smirking.

"Name's Kera. Wanna another drink? God knows, I do."

"Sure. I'll take another Brickhouse."

"Hey, barkeep. Can I get a Brickhouse for the guy and another vodka and cranberry for me?"

"You want it made like the last?" the barkeep asks.

"Yup! You know how I like 'em."

Some time later, the two of you are still dropping quarter after quarter into the game, laughing hysterically as one ridiculous picture supersedes the previous. You've been playing this stupid thing for most of the night, laughing and enjoying the flashback to 80's soft core porn.

After your second beer you decided to switch to Kentucky bourbon so at this point, you're feeling pretty outstanding. You're unsure how many drinks you've had but eh, whatever. Kera has been super cool, paying for just about everything. *It's about time I got taken care of,* you think, remembering how often you've ponied up cash for an entire evening's drinks.

"Hey, whadda ya say we break out of here and hit a club?" Kera asks, tossing her hair back and forth wildly as if she's on the dance floor already. It's very seductive and there's no way in hell you're going to let this one go.

"Sure, let's bounce! My car's just outside, I'll drive."

"That's ok, I can drive. It's no big deal. Besides, you seem like you've had quite a bit to drink."

———————————————

Whatever. She's GOTTA be drunker than you are.
Insist on driving to the club.
Turn to page 16

Acquiesce and let her drive.
Turn to page 150

You jerk the wheel down, spinning the car right. Brakes squeal. The Cadillac slams head first into the Honda. A sickening crunch fills the air as the two front ends meet. Glass shatters and bolts break. The force of the impact pushes your smaller engine through the firewall into the front seat, crushing the two of you rather messily against your seats. You and Loretta are killed instantly.

Whoops.

The End

costume, you strike up a conversation spelling out the pathetic plight you've worked yourself into.

At the end of it, the waitress, seated across from you at this point, merely comments, "Damn. That sucks." *Guess this is not an isolated tale in the gambling capital of the world,* you realize.

"Hey listen," she says. "I got a friend who runs a little marriage chapel a few blocks from here. I work there from time to time. They're looking for a temp hire to fill a job that someone just walked out on. If you're interested, I'm heading there after my shift is over. I bet in a few days you could probably make enough cash to get home. Interested?" Lucinda asks.

With a dearth of options– frankly NO other options– you agree to come along. After a short interview, you're hired. For the next week you work as Elvis alongside Lucinda playing Pricilla, serving as witnesses in lame Rock-N-Roll weddings at the chapel. Your Elvis impression is piss-poor but sure enough, you manage to scrape together enough money to return home, tail between your legs. *Fuck the world.*

The End

Oh Sweet God, I can't believe I'm going to say this. "Um… sure, I guess. Whatever. Just please don't have me arrested. I don't think I can take that."

The old horndog gives you a grandmotherly wink. "Don't worry, sonny. I'll take care of you. Just put yourself in Miss Agatha's hands." You look at her hands and decide that you're not quite sure you're making the right decision.

"Security!" Agatha barks into the radio. "Security, ignore my last request. My old age got the best of me, I'm afraid. I saw a mouse down here and it just about scared the bejeezus out of me. If you get the chance, please call the exterminators to come back."

"Roger that, Agatha. Call exterminators. Sure you're all right?"

Agatha cases your figure, devouring your naked flesh with approving eyes, settling her gaze on the book covering your junk. "Oh yes. I'm doing just fine. Agatha out." Another shudder ripples through your body. The revulsion of what's to come makes your stomach churn.

"Here?" you ask tentatively. "Should we do 'it' here?" You can taste the bile in the back of your throat.

"Oh heavens no. I don't think my old hips can take it on this rough floor. I can still take a good pounding but there's gotta be a little cushion. My seat's not what it used to be." Agatha laughs and turns around, shaking her rear causing ripples to descend along her long woolen skirt.

"We'll go somewhere a little more comfortable. My living facility is right around the corner."

"But, what about my, you know, lack of clothing?"

"Oh don't worry about that. I've got it all covered, so to speak." Agatha titters at her little pun. "Come on, Romeo, there's action to be had," she says as she pinches your cheek and then slaps her butt.

With Agatha's guidance, you make your way back to the service elevator, all the while trying to keep yourself sheltered from the old woman's salacious glances. The two of you board the elevator and you notice that all the quilts are there, one of them slightly stained from last night's romp. Agatha notices you looking at the stained quilt and goes over and pulls it down.

"This should do nicely!" she proclaims as she hands it to you to wrap yourself in. You shudder thinking of what transpired on this quilt and the irony of it being used again toward a most unseemly proposition.

At the lobby, Agatha exits first to see if the coast is clear. Being relatively early still, staff and visitors number few and Agatha motions for you to disembark.

"If you like, we can make it to my condo using a back alley that runs almost the entire way." You nod your obvious agreement. Being cloaked in a cum-stained, dirty quilt is not quite the outfit you were hoping for when exiting the library.

The two of you leave through the same service door that you entered coming into the library, and you dart to the alleyway adjacent to the parking lot. Agatha scurries along behind you, the smile on her face showing that she is evidently enjoying this dirty little escapade. *Goddamn hormone supplements,* you think to yourself as you dash from dumpster to dumpster toward the large, white brick assisted living facility at the alley's mouth ahead.

At the end of the alley, Agatha instructs you to wait for her. You hunker down behind a large pile of trash bags while Agatha goes over to the entrance to get you a visitor's pass. After five minutes, she returns, extremely irate about something.

"Goddamn security says that I can't have visitors up to my condo until ten a.m. I explained that you were my nephew but it didn't matter."

Nephew?! Oh God, that visual just makes this whole situation feel that much more wrong. Ugh. What the hell am I doing?!

Agatha continues, "So listen. This is what we can do. I can't wait until ten. I'm so horny I could hump a broom handle about now. So, what do you say we sneak around to the Scent Garden in back and do it there?" You frown and shake your head. *There is no way you're fucking this old bitch in a public place.* "Fine. I thought you might be a pussy. My friend Bert has a '74 caddy I could get the keys to. How 'bout that? A little shaggin' wagon built for two?"

You sigh, the gravity of what's coming up becoming too much to handle. You've got to think of something and quick.

"Listen Agatha," you say, "there's something VERY sexually arousing about the scent of menthol and old quilts for me. I mean, just wrapping myself in this quilt is already getting my juices flowing. I want to fuck you, Agatha. I want to fuck you like a GI just coming home from WWII. I want to run into those open arms having just killed a slew of Nazis and fuck you like we fucked them. I'm so hot right now, I think I just came a little under this ratty old quilt." You can see this is getting Agatha's blood pressure up and her normal head tremor is becoming more pronounced.

"So, this is what I suggest my little Rosie the Riveter: You go up to your place and get all ready for my homecoming. I want the works. I want your hair done up nice and I want you wearing a Japanese kimono that I can rip off your body like America defiled the Japanese. I want John Phillip Sousa pounding on your Bose radio. I want this Agatha. I want you. I want you now!"

"But how will you get in?" Agatha asks breathlessly, her libido about to explode.

"You leave that up to me, beautiful. You just get ready for my homecoming, ok?"

"I'll be there. I've always been there. I've waited so long for this damn war to end. I want to feel your touch. I want to kiss your lips. I've kept all your love letters. Ten minutes, no more. I can't wait any more than that!"

Agatha turns and waddles quickly across the street into Whitehall's Assisted Living Facility. You exhale a huge sigh of relief and dart back down the alley toward the library. Once you emerge, you quickly make your way around the corner of the massive building to the pay phone. Having no change, you call Thad your roommate collect. You give him strict orders to come immediately and pick you up. You tell him you'll explain everything once he does.

While waiting for Thad, you feel kinda bad for what you did to that poor ol' horny woman. You make a vow that later today you'll tell your grandfather that you've found him a wonderful woman to meet and send him to the library archives with a bouquet of roses and a card for Agatha.

The End

You protest, showing your cuffs to Kera, demanding to have them taken off. She looks slightly confused but decides that maybe you're just playing along, so she grabs a riding crop leaning up against the wall.

CRACK! Kera lashes the riding crop against your thigh, leaving a big welt. She purses her lips and her eyes squint in concentration. **CRACK!** The next swipe lands on your ass. You lurch forward in response. With your feet caught in your jeans, you fall to the floor. You hit hard, unable to catch yourself effectively with your wrists bound.

Barely audible above the industrial grind, you hear Kera scream something angrily at you. **CRACK!** The riding crop falls again, this time on your back. You roll over and hold up your chained wrists, trying to indicate that this is NOT something you're into.

Kera looks at you slightly perplexed. Then with a scolding glance, the riding crop comes down hard on your stomach making you wince.

With some difficulty, you manage to stand up, the riding crop coming down two, three times in the process, leaving various parts of your body searing with pain. You launch yourself at Kera and push her latex clad body against the wall. You lean in and scream at the top of your lungs.

"GET ME THE FUCK OUT OF THESE THINGS! I'M NOT INTO THIS SHIT!"

Kera pushes you forcefully back and then looks over at the two burly men in tight-fitting, black t-shirts standing by the door, nodding her head in your direction. Immediately, one of them comes over and grabs you with his big meaty hands. You struggle against his grip but it's incredibly strong. It's obvious he is in complete control of you. Kicking and wiggling around to get free, you are carried into a back room, and thrown on the floor.

Completely pissed off and ready to kick some ass, you get to your feet only to be knocked unconscious by his sledgehammer of a fist.

At some point later, you wake up next morning with a splitting headache in the doorway to a shop on God knows what street. You look down and notice you're still only wearing your boxers and you are covered in bruises from the riding crop. This sucks.

The End

You pull your head back and look deep into her eyes. You read pure, unrestrained lust and desire. Here, below you, is a gorgeous creature that truly wants you inside of her, to take her with a furious passion. Whatever the tattoo means... who ever 'Margie' is... you could give a flying fuck.

"I could care less abo– " you begin to say in return when frantically Dixie places her finger over your lips, silencing you.

She smiles with both her mouth and eyes. In a low voice she responds, "We have to whisper. It would be <u>really</u> bad to wake my roommate. She's a raging bitch if she gets woken up. Now, let me slip out of my gown and how about you get rid of those pants and tie."

You ease off of Dixie and disrobe quickly and clumsily, your dexterity drained in direct proportion to other aspects that have risen dramatically. Dixie reaches up her back and unzips her gown, letting it fall silently to the floor. A vision of Venus stands naked before you. She steps gracefully over her dress toward you.

You place both hands at her waist and lay her down on the couch. In silence, you passionately make love. The two of you explore a variety of dynamic positions, but it's her muted whimpers that serve to heighten the experience most. Three times you fuck Dixie, each time better than the previous, eventually leaving her a sexual wreck, exhausted and glistening in sweat as the sun breaks through the trees and streams into the apartment.

You stand up and redress in silence, your legs a little weak from the past few hours. As you leave, you turn and take one final glance at the beauty stretched out fully on the couch– nude, her hair a mess, breathing deeply in sleep. You smile as you close the door behind you.

The End

"Alright Mistress of a Million Moves, the ball is in your court. I am your humble student of all that is known and unknown in the world of female sexual pleasure," you say making a mock bow.

"Excellent," Helen replies, pleased with your decision. "Now bottom's up, kid. Let's get out of here." Helen throws the rest of her tumbler full of liquor down her throat. You swirl then swill the rest of yours as well. "Drinks are on me, how about that!" Helen says as she throws down a c-note on the bar, nodding to the bartender.

"Night, Frankie," Helen tosses toward the bar as the two of you leave.

In the parking lot few cars remain, but of those, one clearly stands apart from its cohorts. It's a vibrant red convertible that seats two. Its low-slung chassis and wind-blown lines clearly suggest that it is made to go fast. VERY fast. You slide into the passenger seat and notice that the controls for the car are unlike anything you've ever seen before. On the center console where a gear stick would normally be, four green buttons labeled 'P', 'R', 'D', and 'N' glow. Above them sits a brilliant digital display of the car.

"What exactly is this car? I mean, I see the word 'Tesla' written everywhere, but it means nothing to me."

Helen's eyes gleam with the chance to show off her futuristic ride. "It's a Tesla Roadster. The car is completely electric, hence the 'Tesla' moniker from Nicolas Tesla, inventor of the radio and father of modern day electricity. This baby can go from zero to sixty in 3.7 seconds and has almost three hundred horses under the hood! Needless to say, she rocks the road with a quiet punch. Moreover, her luscious body is modeled after the Lotus Elise, a beautiful automobile in its own right. Ready to go?"

You buckle your seatbelt in anticipation. With hardly a sound, the car's engine comes to life. You turn toward Helen to remark about it, but the car leaves your voice behind as you are thrown back in your seat when Helen slams down the accelerator, kicking out a cloud of tire smoke and loose gravel. You rocket out of the parking lot, slowing down only slightly while turning. The car's grippy tires hug the pavement as the car tightly corners, heading west.

The dramatic acceleration doesn't subside once you enter the city either. Helen's lead foot pushes the Roadster even faster. Buildings blur on either side as they whip by, the car slicing through the atmosphere like a scalpel. With the top down, you can feel a torrential river of wind overhead, lapping at your hair. *Holy shit, she's going fast!* Your pulse races with the exhilaration. You glance over at her, unwilling to take your eyes completely off the road and the certain death that must be coming your way. You smile wanly.

Helen looks over at you and laughs.

"Come on, kid? Don't like to drive fast? What kinda man are you? Seriously though, don't worry. It's a little after two a.m. Honestly, who's going to be out this time of night other than us and some cops that have no chance in Hell catching us?"

You nod your head weakly in agreement and then quickly turn back to watch the road snake under the car at speeds you've never experienced. Flagrantly ignoring any traffic laws, Helen runs red lights, green lights, stop signs... you name it. It's extremely unsettling considering she's been drinking tonight.

You look down at your pants. You hands are grabbing your legs with white-knuckled strength, probably giving you bruises underneath. Furthermore, what was the beginnings of a chubby thinking about all the positions you were going to try tonight has now shrunken to the point where you're pretty sure your outtie has become an innie. *What is this crazy bitch doing?*

Mile after mile screams by as the harrowing minutes pass. *Where the hell are we going?* you think to yourself. Suddenly the car turns into a deserted parking lot and stops– perfectly parked perpendicular to the curb. It takes a second for the buildings to catch up and your stomach to settle. You take a look at the sad storefronts that populate the strip mall around you. In front of you, a dilapidated travel agency rests with dark interior lights. Flaking window paint announces a cruise deal long past.

You look over curiously at Helen. *What the fuck is going on and why the race to get here of all places?* You're kinda starting to wonder if Helen has an ulterior motive in dragging you way past the city to such a deserted island of urban blight. Various thoughts instantly race through your head of possible reasons she might have– most of them bad.

"Um, dare I ask why we're here? I'm guessing you didn't drag me all the way out here to have sex." you say to Helen with a small quiver of trepidation in your voice.

"It's a surprise! I don't want to spoil the surprise."

"Uh… how about we don't make it a surprise? How about instead you tell me why you drove like a bat out of hell to the middle of some burned-out run-down strip mall?" you protest, finding your nuts at last and growing a bit perturbed.

"Let's go into my travel agency, and I promise you'll be taken places you never dreamed were possible."

"What the FUCK does that mean?!" you snap back at her.

"I can't say anymore. Now get out and let's go inside," Helen commands, her voice a mix of directedness laced with a curious urgency.

Go inside with Helen.
Turn to page 260

Refuse.
Turn to page 75

"I think I want you to take me home," you say, adamant about your decision.

"Mmmmm... that's not going to happen," Helen says slowly and reluctantly.

"What? Why? You can't force me to go with you into your creepy travel agency. Now turn around the Batmobile and take me home."

"No." Helen responds simply.

"Fine. Fuck you then, old lady. I didn't want to fuck you anyway. I just felt sorry for your old, wrinkly ass sitting there alone at the bar. I'm out of here," you declare as you open the door and step up and out of the coolest car you've ever ridden in.

"You sure you want to do this?" Helen asks calmly, unphased by your dramatic exit from the car.

"Fuck. You." You turn and start to walk across the parking lot, dodging weeds that have sprung up through cracks in the pavement. *The nerve of her! Just because you have money doesn't mean you own people. Nobody owns me and tells me what to do. Fuck her. Fuck her AND her nice ass car!*

Suddenly from behind, you hear tires squealing, looking for traction amidst the rubble– the sound of Helen backing up in her normal, sensational driving fashion. *Great,* you think sarcastically. You turn to look over your shoulder and see her brake abruptly before gunning the car forward, this time locking the e-brake to fishtail the back wheels around. The car door you left open slams shut with a loud **BAM!** The car sits facing you now, carving out your figure through stark illumination from halogen headlights. *What is she doing?*

You get an uneasy feeling in your stomach and start walking faster across the lot. On the far side is a small thicket of trees that you aim for. The car behind you slowly starts to follow you.

"Are you joking? Listen bitch, I'm gonna make you so moist that rippin' off your panties is gonna be like opening a fuckin' wet nap at a Baptist BBQ. Don't tell me I don't know how to please a woman sexually!" *Nobody takes a potshot at my prowess with the poon!*

"Settle down there, young buck," the cougar says, laughing out loud. "The first thing we need to do is work on your comebacks. A BBQ? Really? Points for creativity, I suppose." She continues to snicker while taking a sip of her cocktail. "Oh, and the name's 'Helen', not 'bitch'," she adds.

She returns her drink to the bar and turns to you. "I'm sorry. I didn't mean to get you all riled up with what I said. How about we settle this with a little quiz of your wisdom on how to please the female form? See if you really know your p's and q's." With a defiant air, you nod your head *Sure*.

"Good. Question one: How do you do a Double Legged Anchor?" Stumped, you shrug your shoulders reluctantly, your face a scowl.

"Bike Pump?" Again, no idea. A frustrated sigh.

"Know about the Boston Brute? The Tangled Spider? The Bronco Buster?" You pause then humbly shake your head "no" for all three. *Dammit. What the hell are all those?*

"Have you at least had a fourgy?" she asks, somewhat sarcastically as if everyone has.

"No." you confess grudgingly. "Well, shit. I haven't done any of those things. I am really good at doggie though!" you throw back at Helen, your voice full of secondhand pride.

"Good. Good for you. You run with that. Anyway, should you want to learn, I'd be willing to teach. How about it, champ? Give it some thought." Helen returns to her drink and nurses it, waiting for you to make the next move.

Too much talking, not enough fucking!
Turn to page 72

She seems a little TOO experienced.
Turn to page 230

"I guess that's just too freakin' bad then, eh? Don't ya git your panties all in a bunch, I'll have ya home soon 'nuf," Carlos replies followed by a gruff little snicker. "Fuggin' patsy."

You sit forward in your seat to bring yourself closer to Carlos. "Seriously, dude. I have to be at work in like three hours to start makin' coffee. I really need to grab some shut eye before then," you plead pathetically.

"Lissen' you little faggut. I've had just about awl I wanna hear from you. Shut yer goddamn mouth and jus sit back. This won't take too long."

You sit back, slightly pissed and a little scared about the "errand" that you are accompanying Carlos to. As a distraction, your mind turns back to the feeling that you've seen this guy before. After minutes of mulling over his name and face, you've still got nothing. You sigh and give up, turning your attention to the dark landscape whizzing by outside.

Then suddenly it hits you. You know where you recognize him from! It's from TV. He's Carlos Pulagatti, a known mob associate and muscle.

You start to sweat and get nauseous, a pit forming deep within your stomach. You can feel your nerves starting to tingle. You look at Carlos again– his beefy neck with greasy, brown hair dripping over his collar. You notice his beady brown rat eyes watching the road, reflected in the rearview mirror. Does he know you recognize him? *Oh shit, oh shit, oh shit*, you think. *Ok. This'll be ok,* you tell yourself. *Just go on the errand, it's all gonna be ok.* Suddenly you notice his eyes are trained on you.

"Hey! You's ok back there? Yer getting' all figity. You gotta pee or sumthin'?" his thick Brooklyn accent hammering your ears.

"Um… yeah. I gotta pee. Like real bad, man. Can we pull off and find a gas station or something?"

"Shit. Ok," he says reluctantly. "Fuggin' pussy bladder," he comments quietly under his breath.

The palatial Town Car pulls off the interstate at the next exit and into a brightly lit gas station, right in front of the men's room. You jump out of the car and rush for the bathroom, really trying to sell how bad you need to go. Once inside, you lock the door and dial 911. *Fuck!* It's a piss-poor connection laced with static and dropouts. You initially try to whisper your plea for help but with the crappy connection you inadvertently begin talking very loudly in order to get the operator to hear you.

"Who da FUCK are you tawking to!"

Suddenly, a loud pounding shakes the door. You scream into the phone that you need help, right FUCKING now.

With a loud crash, the door comes off its top hinge and swings into the bathroom. Carlos comes barreling in, snatches the phone from your hand and throws it into the stained toilet nearby. He grabs you and heaves you violently against the shabby cinder block wall. You slam your head, blurring your vision. A loud sandy scrape follows and as you turn, the blur of white porcelain streaks through the air, coming down with a thick, meaty **CRACK** as it bashes your head in.

Obviously annoyed, Carlos unceremoniously dumps your dead body in the Lincoln's trunk on top of a shovel and bag of lime he always carries back there for times like these. He closes the trunk, relights his stump of a cigar and puffs greedily, mulling over burial spots.

The End

You lean toward Kera whose dancing is a mix of epilepsy and kung fu. With all the air in your lungs, you scream, "I'LL BE RIGHT BACK." She doesn't even notice. You shrug your shoulders and shake your head. You can feel your gorge rising so there's no time to try again.

You push your way thought the writhing crowd, frantically searching for something that looks like a bathroom door. You jump up, trying to get above the crowd; although, all you can see is sweeping lights illuminating the seething masses surrounded in a pitch black shell.

You press on, breathing faster, your mouth starting to water. *Oh shit. I better find–* Your thought is interrupted as your stomach has decided not to wait any longer. You lean over, elbows on knees and heave out a prodigious amount of vomit. A few dancers notice and frown but no one stops dancing, dismissive of the puke they are splashing over their shoes.

You feel much better and decide to give this night one last chance. You fight your way back to Kera who doesn't even seem to have noticed your absence.

Over the next couple of hours, you release yourself to your surroundings, letting the anger of the music sweep over you. The angst, the grinding metal, the incredibly fast pulsing beat– these elements fill you with an overwhelming feeling of hate. By the end of the night you find yourself enraged by the stupidity of mankind, specifically your fucking boss, and all those that have wronged you since the day you were born. Your adrenaline surges as you dance faster and faster, railing against the world.

With a passion you have never felt before, you reach out, seize Kera and kiss her violently, biting down on her lip with such force you draw blood. You grab her around the waist, she around your neck, and you kiss over and over again, the animal inside raging from the cacophony around you.

The two of you locked together push violently through the crowd, unconcerned where you are heading, focused only the sexual energy welling up between you. At the edge of the crowd, you slam Kera forcefully against the cloth-covered wall of the club. You grab her hair, brutally kissing her.

Your bodies pump in time to the music. You hoist Kera up and rip off her underwear from under her skirt. Her nails dig into your shoulders. She undulates back and forth, her body screaming to be penetrated. You clumsily jerk down your pants and the two of you have animalistic sex right there against the curtain. Kera screams in ecstasy and scratches your back as the two of you gyrate to the beat. You lose complete track of time, only reentering reality when you've climaxed.

You pull back slightly and look at Kera who is licking her lips, her big eyes trained on you. She leans in, softly biting your earlobe and whispers seductively, "Again."

The End

"You go for it, then. Knock yourself out," you challenge Julie sarcastically.

Julie smiles, and stands up. "Watch and learn, Romeo. Watch and learn." She then saunters up to the bar, giving you one last look over her shoulder, smirking. You finish your drink with one final gulp and hit the call button on your table to signal the stewardess to come by.

Meanwhile up at the bar, Julie is working her magic. She has ordered a beer and is gently nursing it. She sits down at a barstool near a gorgeous woman who is much taller than her. (You like tall!) The woman has long, chestnut brown hair that is expertly styled suggesting she's on the market.

Chicks and their hair– for Chrissake, you'll never understand that relationship. This one girl you dated in college for a while would get up like a whole hour earlier in the morning to do her hair. What's more, fuckin' bitch used to wake you up with that goddamn hairdryer of hers. *Hell, it was more of a jet turbine than a hairdryer. That relationship sure didn't last long.*

Whoa, what's this?! You snap back to the present when you notice Julie laughing with the brunette, putting her hand on the woman's knee, seemingly to steady herself. *Way to sell the drunk angle, Jules!*

Julie points at you from across the bar. *That's right, play me up, baby!* You strike your most Brat Pack pose with your newly refreshed drink, attempting to look like a devilish Dean Martin or a suave Frank Sinatra. You idly stare off into the distance as if drinking at the club is an everyday affair to wind down the day.

Before you know it, Julie has brought her new acquaintance back to the table. Responsibly, she has barely drunk one-fifth of her beer, using it mostly as a prop during her conversation.

"This is Ginnie," Julie says, introducing the brunette.

"Nice to meet you," Ginnie says with a grin. "Julie has told me tons about you."

"Did she?" you say putting on your most surprised-looking face. "Julie's a real peach."

"Oh, I can tell. She's got the most endearing sense of humor," Ginnie says flashing a smile at Julie.

The three of you talk and laugh, tossing back drinks like a runner slamming water after a race. You're having a great time talking to Ginnie. She's so friendly, constantly poking Julie when she says something funny. *God, she's gorgeous! This is all working so well.* Ginnie sits next to Julie, giving you the opportunity to occasionally reach out with a furtive foot and play a little footsie with her under the table. She's obviously a little shy since she has yet to play back, just returning a confused smile at your attempts.

Close to 1 a.m., Julie announces that she's getting tired and she's ready to go. Ginnie promptly asks if she might get a ride home, saving her a bit in cab fare. *Fuck yeah! This is perfect!*

Without pausing for Julie to respond, you pipe up. "Of course! You're totally welcome to come with us!"

Ginnie's exceedingly grateful. She looks at Julie who just laughs and shrugs her shoulders. "You heard the man. Looks like you're coming back with us!" The two of them giggle, you're not sure about what; but hey, it's what chicks do.

The three of you pile into Julie's car, you in the back and the two girls up front. You hunker forward between the seats to stay in the conversation. The three of you talk about life, the future and what you're going to be when you "grow up"–aspirational crap. Julie seems to be a little reserved for some reason, but then again it's late, so maybe she's just tired.

Ginnie turns around, her arm using Julie's seat as a brace to turn further. "So, should we drop you off first or are you up for a little ride to my house?"

Hmmm. That's a good question, you think. *Would it be better to get dropped off first and see if she wants to come in? Is she the kinda girl that'd see that as forward? Or, would it be better to ride to her house and make a move there, maybe inviting yourself up for a nightcap and... perhaps a little sexy-time?*

———————————

Ask to be dropped off first.
Turn to page 211

Tell them you're fine to ride along to Ginnie's house.
Turn to page 212

Alrighty. Pete it is, you decide. You look back on some of your more dubious romantic encounters and think how much you really could have used someone to keep you on the straight and narrow. *God knows,* you think, *I've banged enough ugly chicks while drunk to foster a generation of unattractive people and set about a charisma recession in the gene pool. Pete's gonna be a good choice.* You give him a call.

"Hey Petey! How's it hangin'? Wanna go out tonight and hit on chicks?" you ask.

"Sure. I guess that sounds kinda fun. Although, listen. I don't want to go to some sleazy slut joint like last time. I swear to God, I saw more used condoms in the parking lot than cigarette butts. It was gross."

"Sure, sure," you reply. "How about I let YOU pick the place then this time. My only request is that it's gotta be somewhere I can be all dolled up since I'm sporting the suit and tie tonight, dig?"

"Okay. No problem. Hmmmm... classy and not too full of whores–"

You interrupt Pete. "Whoa whoa! Nothing wrong with a few whores there, bud. I mean, I sure as shit don't want to go to a foo-foo wine bar and hit on soccer moms."

"Ok, ok. I got ya. I know, let's hit the Landing Strip, the lounge out by the airport. It's got some great jazz music and I'm sure there are some swanky swingers to be had with all the business hotels in the area. And hey horndog, if you get lucky, you can fuck your brains out in a nearby hotel room."

Airport bar? Really? You sigh and roll your eyes. *Maybe inviting dorky Pete wasn't the greatest idea.* You're starting to have some regrets. *Oh well. The Landing Strip isn't the best idea but at least he's right that there will be plenty of well-dressed business ladies to hook up with.* Hell, maybe you can even give one or two of 'em a souvenir fuck as a memento.

"Ok bud. The Landing Strip it is. I'll be at your place in forty-five minutes." You hang up, brush your teeth and get in the car.

Once on the highway, you rifle through your cds and throw in your "Getting Laid" mix, an assortment of pre-game stadium songs to get your blood pumping and your confidence building. Soon you're pounding on the steering wheel to the music, all psyched to get this evening started.

You pull up in front of Pete's place forty minutes later and turn down the music slightly before Pete gets in.

"Oh shit, is this your 'Fuck Mix' again?" Pete asks. "Do we have to listen to this <u>every</u> time we go out?"

You feel a little predictable but reply, "Hell yeah, dude! Bein' a pimp is a state of mind!" Pete just rolls his eyes.

"Hey, I called you while you were driving over to see if you wanted me to reserve a table since it's usually crowded, but you didn't pick up. I guess you couldn't hear your phone over the music."

You instinctually reach down to your pocket to see if your phone shows a missed call. Uh oh, your phone isn't there. You pat your other pocket but no luck there either. You've forgotten your cell. *Dammit! It's too far to drive back and get it, too. Oh well, whatever.* You're with your most responsible friend. He'll take care of you if the shit hits the fan.

Turn to page 275

Decision made, you proclaim with gusto: "Right on ladies, let's head! I'm ready to practice the Mockbar with the betclef, or whatever the fuck it's called!"

Pete just rolls his eyes. "Sorry ladies, I'm out for tonight. I'm gonna have to jet. I have an early morning tomorrow. Take care of this one, he's a bit of a stallion if you know what I mean, and a little drunk to boot. *JachchoHmeH 'Iwraj penaghtaH.*"

The two girls giggle. You look at Pete dumbfounded, but he just smiles and leaves the three of you. Together, you stumble drunkenly back to the girls' room. It's a fun walk, with plenty of stumbling and bumbling along the way.

Once inside their suite, you plop down on the bed, as if exhausted from the walk over. The two women tower over you like Amazons. They exchange glances and announce that they would like to slip into something more conducive for the evening ahead. *Oh hell yeah.*

"Be my guest, ladies. Just don't leave me here too long. I'm ready to do some battle with my bigheft!"

The two ladies leave to change. Meanwhile, you strip down to your sexy bikini underwear, stoked that you dressed well for what's to come. Almost naked, you climb back on the bed and strike your best male porn pose.

Not long thereafter, the two ladies come back and oh my God, have they changed! Both are clad head to toe in some sort of weird battle armor. In addition, they have on brown, ridged skullcaps affixed to their foreheads. Their skin has been darkened with makeup to match their new headpieces. On their side dangle wicked, metallic swords in a crescent shape with four points. You react.

"Holy fucking shit! What the hell is going on? Why the fuck are you dressed like that and what the fuck is that sword thingy?!"

"Silence, toDSaH! I am 'ech Kerla," the hitherto meek Dutch woman declared.

"And I am HoD SepIch. The weapons you see are the *bat'leth* I spoke of. Are you prepared to be a *par'mach*?"

Honestly, you're not really sure what to do. You're obviously in over your head here, sitting dumbstruck in your ridiculous bikini underwear being confronted by two well-built, unbalanced women dressed as Klingons hellbent on doing something to you– something that will most likely hurt. This is not quite what you had in mind and suddenly you realize how stupid this whole encounter must look.

You sigh and resign yourself to the madness of the situation you've found yourself in.

"Sure. Fuck it. Do your worst, 'ech Kerla and HoD SepIch." You smile and lie back on the bed, spread eagle, waiting for what will happen next.

'ech Kerla looks at HoD SepIch, smiles a wicked smile and together, they change your life.

*   *   *   *

Looking back, that was a one helluva night! The two Klingon battle chicks tied you up and the three of you had a very physical, some might say violent, *ménage à trois*. There was lots of Klingon cursing and while it was surreal, it was off the hook. Ten years have passed since that night, and it remains a highlight in your sexual history.

"Hey, Sa' B'Etor! Did you say you want another glass of *Chech'tluth*?" your wife asks.

You turn to her. Your wife is dressed in full Klingon battle regalia standing at the bar, her long cape flowing out behind her. Her gorgeous, knotted forehead blends perfectly with her face which is painted to match the latex headpiece. You smile at her and then remembering, scowl. You place your hand on the plastic *bat'leth* that hangs at your side and bark, "Insolent *toh-pah*, do not make me repeat my order."

Your wife winks at you and purchases the two drinks. She then comes over and the two of you crash your glasses together to celebrate your tenth anniversary of attending StarCon. Bottoms up!

The End

Ok, ok. You could've gone for the gun, but honestly, who are you kidding. You're not some action hero from the movies and in such a tight area, there are tons of things that could go wrong.

The massive smokestacks of factories loom on the horizon, dark splotches against an even darker night as you continue farther south. Unsure of where you are going and what they plan to do to you once you get there, you feel your heart beating loudly in your chest. Your hands quake so you grip them together to keep from being so visibly afraid.

You turn your head and look out the window, wondering if this will be the last time you will ever see the stars. Just then a pain shoots through your leg. You jerk your head around to find the woman removing a syringe from your thigh. You've been injected with something! Poison? Some truth drug? *I don't even know anything worth telling!*

"What the hell? What was that?" you ask although the answer comes from your own body as you feel yourself getting infinitely tired.

"Don't worry. I've just injected you with a sedative. Can't be having you seeing where your nation keeps its secrets, can we?" the woman answers in a soothing voice.

"Secrets? What seeeee…" That's about all you manage to say before you pass out completely.

When you awaken, you're lying face down on your front lawn. Your head hurts like hell, and you're unsure if it's because of all the alcohol you consumed last night or the after effects of whatever shit you were injected with. You roll over and the morning sun blinds you momentarily. You sit up and look down at yourself to see if everything's ok.

You open your suit coat to find that on your shirt, over your right breast, is a round sticker with a bald eagle on it, clutching arrows in one claw and an olive branch in the other. Emblazoned across the eagle in bright red blocky letters reads: *I'm a Good Citizen*!

The End

Sorry Thad.

"My car's parked outside," you say. You lead the way to your car– a big disappointment in Foxy's book. It's clear your current riceburner is a far cry from the bitchin' V6, four on the floor Chevy ride she was craving. Clear of the club, you're privately hopeful that maybe Foxy will shed her 1970's world for the current decade.

The two of you get in and Foxy gives you directions to her pad. Settling in for the ride, Foxy sheds her golden pumps and puts both feet up on the dash. She then pulls a long thin cigarette from the pack in her purse and punches in the car's cigarette lighter. After a few moments, it pops back out. Never having been used, the cigarette lighter infuses the car with the faint odor of burning plastic. Foxy withdraws the glowing plug and sparks up, inhaling deeply. You roll down your window some since it's obvious that Foxy has no intention of doing so.

"So Machine Gun Joe," Foxy starts, "what do you think of the President?"

"I dunno. I guess he's doing a pretty good job. I mean, I really don't follow politics much; but you know, whatever."

"Are you kidding me?!" Foxy responds. "That fascist pig is responsible for this police state we live in! Fucking Christ! The President and his Frankenstein goon are reprehensible! Seriously man, we need to do something about it. You more than anybody should know that second place sucks." Foxy is clearly all worked up, and you're a little worried talking about such a hot topic with her after having just met her.

"Well… huh. I guess I never thought–" Before you can complete your lame, milktoast response, Foxy suddenly leans over and jerks the wheel, sending the car careening toward a pedestrian on the sidewalk.

"What the fuck!" you scream as you overpower her to regain control of the car. You swerve wildly, narrowly missing the poor guy who has to throw himself against the wall in order to stay alive.

"Dammit Machine Gun, you're gonna lose the race if you don't start trying! Don't worry though. I think with you and me as a team, Frankenstein is going to get a run for his spot." Foxy responds with confidence. She then goes back to smoking her cigarette, staring idly out the window.

You're pretty shaken up by the near miss and are not at all sure what the hell she's talking about. Thank God, the car ride is over as you pull up and park on the street in front of her house.

Turn to page 117

You pick up a fry and dip it into the Franch, fully coating the tip of the fry. You look with mock trepidation at the fry and then at Kitty.

"Ohhhh-kay. Here goes nothing." You take a bite.

OH MY GOD! you think as soon as the fry hits your tongue. Immediately, your stomach churns, and you feel your whole body recoil from the taste. You frantically reach for a napkin to spit it into, but before you can even grab one, the complete contents of your stomach splash all over a smiling Kitty and the technicolor floor at her feet. Your throat burns horribly.

"You fucking asshole! What the fuck!" Kitty screams at you.

"Oh my God," you apologize frantically, "I am so sorry. I didn't mean to. It was a knee-jerk reaction to the Franch. Oh Jesus. It was just so bad! Let me help you clean yourself off." You grab the napkins you were so desperate to reach earlier and hand them to her in a pathetic show of assistance. "At least, let me pay for your dry cleaning."

Kitty looks at you, ferocity blazing in her eyes stemming from the vomit covering her pants and the over-the-top rejection of one of her favorite foods.

"You know, here's an idea. Why don't you go FUCK YOURSELF while I go to the bathroom and try to get your FUCKING PUKE off of me!" Kitty storms off.

You wipe the last bit of Franch critique off your chin and try to recompose yourself. You straighten your tie and wince at the pain in your gut. *God, what the hell was in that dipping sauce?!* You feel horrible. *It's time to go. Screw this.*

Your stomach tied up with shooting pains, you make your way to the dance floor searching for Thad. You find him gettin' down with the woman in pink, moving like it's 1978 all over again.

"Dude!" you scream, wincing from the shooting pain the effort causes. "Dude, let's go! I wanna go!"

Thad hears your voice but continues to dance. He shoots you a withering look while shaking his head slightly, clearly saying *Not now! Things are working out well with this chick.* You respond by making the universal sign for vomiting by jerking your head forward while sticking out your tongue. Thad just looks at you confused then gives you the head nod to screw off and wait for him at the bar.

You wince again with the next shooting pain and shuffle over to the bar. You order a ginger ale to try and calm your stomach, but it doesn't help much. You lightly sip it every few minutes until it's completely watered down from the melted ice. *This sucks,* you say to yourself, as the time ticks by until Thad finally makes his way over to you almost an hour later.

You succinctly explain what happened with Kitty. Thad just laughs.

"Dude, that sucks! I'm sorry to hear that your night was so shitty. Well listen, why don't you drive yourself home and

get into bed. I think Foxy and I are going back to her place.
Don't wait up for me, I may not be home till tomorrow."
Thad winks and elbows you which doesn't help the situation.

You snatch the keys from him and walk away, one hand
pressing in on your side in an attempt to help control the
pain. *Asshole. That should have been me getting some play
tonight. Goddamn Franch dressing.*

The End

"You suuuuuure? They're REEEEEEEALLY good!" Kitty pesters you.

Oh ok. Why the hell not.
Turn to page 102

No thanks. Really, I'm good.
Turn to page 190

You steel yourself and go with what works. You set your switch to JERK and stroll over to the bombshell, clearly pompous in your swagger.

"Hey gorgeous. So lemme ask you, what sorta fuckin' sissy drink are you guzzling there?" Before she can answer, you grab the drink, make a disdainful look, and pour it out on the stylish carpet below. "How about you stop drinking those sorority girl drinks, and drink something more befitting someone with a little class?"

"Excuse me? What the fuck is your problem?" The woman is clearly more pissed and annoyed than awestruck by your action.

"What's going on here, baby? Is this man annoying you?" A large woman, hitherto unnoticed by you, standing by the blonde speaks up with an edge in her husky voice.

"This piece of shit here just poured out my drink! And to top it off, I think the prick got some of it on my Diane von Furstenberg dress!"

Addressing the large woman directly, "Excuse me sir, but I believe this is between the lady and I." You turn to the blonde, "I apologize, but I just can't quietly abide watching people of our caliber" you gesture to yourself and the blonde, "drink swill such as that. Action had to be taken. Now sir," you turn your attention back to the beefy woman, "if you will go back to your Miller High Life and stop bothering the lady, it would be much appreciated."

"Excuse me?" the large woman asks. She has close-cropped hair and wears an ill-fitting pantsuit with a short jacket. Her simple white blouse underneath opens up to reveal <u>enormous</u> breasts. "You better not be talking to me like that. I'm liable to pop you one, jerk." She turns to the blonde. "C'mon Dixie, let's move away from this fucktard."

"Dixie?!" you say with mock surprise to the blonde, your voice dripping with sarcasm. "Your name is 'Dixie'? Were you named after a grocery store or the family dog? Seriously, a good looking woman like you can NOT have a name as trite as that. How about I'll call you 'Eleanor', a much more befitting name. Now, if you please, send your bull-dyke friend away so we can get on with our night, and I can buy you a proper beverage."

You turn to the large woman on the opposite side of Dixie and say drolly, "Listen butch, Dixie and I would like some privacy, so why don't you go back to scoping chicks at the other end of the bar and dream of all the doughnut bumping you're NOT going to be doing later. Buh bye."

A redness creeps up the woman's face, and her fists clench in anger. Were she a cartoon, you could easily imagine steam coming out from her protruding nostrils which are flaring like shutters in a windstorm.

"That's it. You're gonna get what you deserve."

"Now Marge, calm down," Dixie chimes in. "He's not worth it. Don't let this asshole be the cause of your return."

You are a little confused by Dixie's comment. *A return to what?* you wonder. No sooner do you ask yourself the question than Marge answers it. She removes her jacket and exposes bulky arms covered by prison tats, the most prominent of which reads the name "Dixie".

Ohhhhh fuck. This bitch has done time! You really have bitten off more than you could chew. You start to instinctually back away, apologizing for dumping Dixie's drink and your poorly phrased comments about Marge's sexual orientation. You don't get far when Marge's mitts grab you roughly by the lapels of your jacket and pull you in close for a beating.

The next twenty minutes are the worst ass beating you have ever received. Pounding fists rain down around you, breaking your nose and blackening both eyes. At one point, Marge even slams your face into the bar, knocking out at least three teeth. Nobody at the bar steps in– all of the patrons are stunned by the brutal scene unfolding in front of them.

At the conclusion of it, you are left crumpled on the floor, a few ribs broken by the kicking right there at the end.

Dixie and Marge quickly leave when sirens peel through the still air of the bar.

Note to self: Asshole approach <u>not</u> effective with lipstick lesbians.

The End

Suddenly sober, you realize you need to leave, and NOW! You glance at the door and realize there's no way in hell you're going to make it without Marge getting within arm's reach of you and doing God knows what. *Shit. Well, if it's not going to be the door, I guess it's going to have to be the window,* you decide.

You bounce up off the couch and turn toward the large window. Your unbuttoned pants sag down, exposing your bikini briefs further. You reach for the sash only to find it locked tight.

"Whatcha doin' there, boy-o? You wouldn't think of leaving the party now, would you?" Marge asks you mockingly from across the room. Dixie hits her playfully on the tummy.

"Now you stop that, Margie. Be nice. We were just playing!"

"That's not what it sounded like to me, Dix. I think the horndog over there was trying to fuck you. And nobody fucks you, but me."

"Oh Margie-wargie, why are you so mean to all my friends?"

During their ridiculous interchange, you manage to find the latch keeping the window closed, but it appears to be painted shut. *Fuck!* You settle for the next best thing. You reach down, grab a pillow from the couch and hold it against the plate glass. With your other hand, you pull back and punch through the pillow, shattering the glass with a loud **CRASH!**

The glass explodes outwards onto the fire escape, huge pieces falling through the metal grate to the sidewalk below, tinkling as they shatter in the distance.

"What the FUCK do you think you're doing?!" Marge screams out and leaps across the room toward you. With one hand, you pull your sagging pants up as high as you can. You highstep from the couch over the remaining angular shards jutting dangerously toward your crotch. God, if you slip, you could easily sever a major artery in your leg and bleed out in

The platform vibrates with the arrival of Marge's first boot, a high-laced black face-stomper frequently worn by skin heads and punks, a dark portent of her arrival. Marge, her arm covered in blood dripping like a leaky faucet from her hand, steps through the shattered window. Her thick black cargo pants push through the glass, breaking it off en route. Dixie grips her other arm, pathetically attempting to hold her in the apartment.

"Don't go anywhere there, boy. I'm going to show you what Hell looks like!" Marge calls out to you.

"Margie honey, don't. He's not worth it! I love you, honey!" Dixie pleads.

Panicked, you sit on the edge of the gaping hole, ready to drop to the hard ground below. You pray that maybe you'll only roll your ankle and not break anything. You then realize that maybe you can lessen the distance somewhat with your shirt!

You rip your shirt off your body, an easy task with all the buttons missing. You tie a huge knot in one sleeve and rapidly push the other sleeve through the grate beside where you sit. The arrival of the second boot shakes the platform. *It's now or never. Here's hoping the knot holds!*

You spin and dive head first through the hole, both hands grabbing the sleeve underneath the platform. You summersault in the air, your body unfolding toward the pavement as your shirt stops your fall, swinging you backwards. Fully extended now, the length of your shirt coupled with the length of your body, your feet dangle only about seven feet from the pavement. You release your grip and drop to the concrete below.

Instinctively, you turn and look up at Marge and the red rain spilling from her arm to the ground near you. Furious rage spills from her mouth, a tirade of swear words and actions dreamt up only by serial killers and demons. Your mind reels trying to comprehend even a tenth of the horrible things she's planning to do to you.

Temporarily safe, you dart away into the early morning–running as fast and as long as you can to put as much distance as possible between you and Marge. You run and run and run, not daring to look back. After who knows how long, you stop to catch your breath. With a fair amount of searching, you manage to locate a payphone, a real rarity in this age of cell phones, and call your roommate collect.

"Hey Thad, I'm really sorry to wake you, but I could really use a ride. It's been one helluva night. And hey, could you bring me some pants?"

The End

"You know, it's no wonder that people have such problems with percents in America. Take this example: Compare a four cylinder car and a six cylinder car. A car with six cylinders has 50% more cylinders than a four cylinder car; however, if you flip it around, a four cylinder car has 33% less cylinders than a six cylinder car. Crazy, huh? What the hell is going on? Is it 50% or 33%? It really all depends on your frame of reference, ya know, just like Einstein's theory of relativity."

The woman has stopped mid-drink and is just staring at you. She purses her lips together and squints her eyes a bit. She subtly nods her head but says nothing. *Did I impress her?* you wonder. *Chicks dig a smart guy, right?* The slow nodding continues. Finally, she responds.

"Ok wow. That's... hmmm... fascinating. You obviously have your finger on the pulse of America," she says with dripping sarcasm. "I think I need to go."

With that, she pulls a twenty dollar bill from her purse, places it beneath the half-finished drink and walks out without looking back. *Shit.* You kick the bar.

Ok...note to self: Chicks don't like a know-it-all showoff.

The End

You decide that looking nice is important, but a suit just makes you look too much like some business guy prick. *Better to go with a more hip look that says I care about what I look like, but I'm not all stuffy and self-important.* Moreover, there are only so many places to go where a suit is appropriate.

You look over your closet. *Hmmmm... definitely nice jeans, they go with just about anything.* You reach for a pair of boxers to put on first, but then realize that your only nice pair of jeans is a close-fitting, dark wash number that doesn't play well with boxers. They get all bunchy, and shit doesn't sit right with that combo. Rather than appear to be fondling yourself all night, shifting the General and his troops to and fro, you pull down a pair of whitey-tighties from the shelf and slip 'em on. *Besides, it's never a bad idea to keep the boys in close.*

You grab your jeans and pull them on too, grabbing a brown leather belt to add to your developing look. To finish your outfit, you choose a nice plain black t-shirt and a brown tweed suit coat. *The jeans say 'mellow' and the coat says 'money'.* Dark socks and nice shoes– you're good. You check yourself out in the mirror. *Most excellent.*

Last up, you hit the bathroom to wet your hair and give it a bit of a wild look with some gel. You also brush your teeth. *God, nothing is worse than hitting on a chick and having her recoil from the stank coming out of your mouth.*

Fresh breath and suited up, you are <u>ready</u> for the ladies. *They have NO idea what's gonna hit 'em!* Putting your toothbrush back, you look in the bathroom mirror and mull over the evening's options.

You certainly don't want to fuck up your first night out in quite a while by being hasty and ending up drunk and alone, so best to draw up a strategy before you get this safari started. A thousand questions explode in your head all at once like a firework overhead on the Fourth. *Where to go? Should I bring a wingman? If so, who?*

"Hey Lille! Looks like it's time for me to jet but I wanted to let you know that I had a really great time tonight and I'd love to see ya again sometime!"

Confused and a little put off by your rush to the table, Lille responds, "Yeah, uh… sure. I mean, I had a great time too. What's your phone number? I'll call you."

"Excellent. My number is 5… 2… 4… 6… 1… UGH!" Suddenly you're roughly tackled from behind by bodyguard number two who comes out of nowhere.

"Taste the smackdown of all-conference, bitch! We've called the police and you're history!" the bodyguard proclaims proudly to the back of your head.

You pull your face up off the floor and crane your neck as high as it will go. "Mmmphh. 6… 1… 7… 7…"

"Wait. Wait. 5. 2. 4. 6… what? What was the next number? 3?!" Lille yells back to you.

"No. 5… 2… 4… 6… 1… 7… SevYOUCH!" you say hurriedly, correcting her until your arm is twisted up behind your back in a classic police hold.

"Ok. 5. 2. 4. 6. 1. 7. 9? Is that what you said? Nine? I didn't understand you."

"No Goddammit!" You respond angrily while you are being forcefully pulled off the floor. "It's 5… 2… 4… 6… 1… 7… SEVEN… 2… 5!"

"Don't shout at me! I can't remember things when people shout at me." Lille complains.

Before you can apologize, you're manhandled to the front of the club where sure enough, the police are waiting to take you away. You are booked an hour later for being drunk and disorderly and taken to a holding cell.

Inside, you pass out and manage to sleep for a little while. However, at four a.m. you're roused when the public toilet in the cell backs up, unleashing a flood of toilet paper, shit and loud complaints from the other inmates. It takes what seems like an eternity to clean it up and by then, the massive hangover you knew was inevitable has started to set in.   Finally around 10 a.m., your roommate Thad shows up and bails you out.

"Thanks dude, I totally owe you one," you say weakly to Thad, the pounding in your head reaching epic levels. "Hey, do you have any aspirin?"

"No dude, sorry." *Ugh, strike one for the new day.*

You pull out your phone and turn it on, a little chime gleefully telling you it's powering up. *Goddamn happy phone.* The phone beeps, telling you you have a text.

Fun night!   Thankx for the invite!   You'll never guess who I fuk'd!–B

Great! I spend the night in jail, Brandi gets lucky. Strike two for the new day.

You start to text her back when you feel your gorge rising. *Crap.* Strike three. You puke all over your nice shoes.

The End

"Obviously I would expect you to say something like that being part of the Underground," Foxy retorts angrily. "Besides, why would I ever want to leave here? When my lifeclock blinks and LastDay finally arrives, I know I will be renewed. Goodbye, Runner."

With those cryptic parting words, Foxy shoots you dead.

The End

"Fuck that dude, I'm not gay. I'm trying to be cool here with you bein' all queer and shit, but I have to draw the line. I am NOT putting on a dress, wig and heels. Uh uh. No way, no how. At least if those assholes catch me, I'll look good on my way to the hospital– good and <u>male</u>, thank you. Thanks, but no thanks. Cross-dressing is NOT going to solve this problem of ours."

At the end of your little diatribe, as if on cue, the pickup comes tearing down the exit ramp of the parking garage, back towards you.

"Shit!" you both say in unison. You drop the dress and Loren drops the wig and shoes, quickly slamming the trunk closed as the two of you race to get back into the car.

Loren turns the key, bringing the Honda back to life. He reaches down, slams the shifter in reverse and turns to look over his shoulder as he backs up.

It's too late though. The Honda gets only a few inches before it is boxed in by the truck which comes to a screeching halt directly behind the car. You're not going anywhere.

You can feel the fear rising up inside of you as you turn to see two huge goons get out, both wearing white cowboy hats and carrying baseball bats. You panic, not knowing what to do. Are you safer in the car? Should you get out and make a run for it? Maybe you can pay them off. Maybe they'll only intimidate you, break a few bones and not kill you.

Your moment of indecision lasts too long as both doors fly open simultaneously and you and Loren are dragged from the car. Dammit, if you had only buckled your seatbelt! You could have had more time to do…something.

You are thrown forcefully on the ground and kicked hard. You know your only chance now is to get up and run like hell. So with every ounce of willpower, you thrust yourself up to sprint away. As you rise though, the bat sings through the air and cracks you in the center of your back. Pain lances through your body as the force of the swing drives you down on to your face. You slam into the pavement, missing any opportunity to catch yourself. Your face digs into the gravel of the decaying cement.

You roll over, your body protesting while the next swing connects with your upper arm. Bone shatters internally and you scream out, instinctively clutching the smashed area with your other hand. A scream from Loren joins yours. Your voices dance back and forth as one blinding blow follows another, slowly crushing your two bodies. Loren's last whimper fades away and you finish the beating solo until you finally black out.

In the end, your wish to be good and male, dressed to impress on your way to the hospital, comes true. Unfortunately, you never wake up to realize it. You're dead– killed by hillbillies. Your obituary laments the death of you and your lover who were killed in a hate crime.

The End

"No, I'm sorry. It's been a long night and I just want to be alone right now. I'm sure you can understand."

"Listen, Sir. I sympathize with your desire to get the hell out of here, but I honestly can't wait for another cab. Anything I could do to change your mind?"

"No," you say. "No, I'm sorry."

"Then I guess I am too." From her coat pocket, the woman pulls a small gun that couldn't hold more than a few rounds. Your eyes widen. You've never actually had a real gun pointed at you. *What the fuck is going on here?* "I think we both need to catch this cab. Shall we get in?"

"Um… that's ok," you respond fearfully. "It's all you. It's your cab. Please take it with my compliments."

"That ship has sailed. Get in."

The two of you enter the cab. Upon closing the door, the driver turns around and smiles.

"Nice to see you again, Margaret. What, it's been five years maybe?"

"Morning James. Thanks for the ride. The cab's a nice touch." You just stare at them both, completely dumbfounded about what's going on. The cab lurches forward and departs the airport complex. You start freaking out as you're being held at gunpoint, going God knows where in a shitty ass taxi.

"Uhhhh… if it's all the same, could you just drop me off somewhere? Anywhere? I can catch a bus, no problem. Seriously, it's totally fine by me. Anywhere is fine. Here is fine. I'm not picky."

"Sorry bub, you're shit outta luck on that one," the driver answers. Disheartened, you sit back and stare at the back of the driver's seat, panicking about what's to come.

From the airport, the taxi turns toward an industrial complex south of the city. Your mind immediately jumps to all the scenes you've seen in the movies where you'll be tortured, cut apart, thrown in a vat of acid to dissolve or sealed in a fifty-five gallon drum with nuclear waste– the list is endless.

glowing suds. Surrounding the club is a parking lot the size of a small nation. Amazingly enough, almost the whole lot is full and it's a challenge to find a space.

"See dude, I don't disappoint," Kevin notes when the car is parked. "This place is going to be fuckin' off the hook with bitches all up in our jocks. You gotta believe all these stripper chicks are strung out on blow, so throw around a little cash, buy 'em a few drinks... I've got no doubt that by closing time we'll be rockin' this shitmobile till the struts blow out."

"Fuck you dude, this 'shitmobile' is a fine car."

"No bro, I didn't mean that. I mean– hell, I don't even got a car, so it's all good. Listen, let's head in and get this night started."

"Yeah dude, good to go."

The two of you get out and head to the door of the club. You open it and pulsing stripper music disrupts the silence of the night.

_____

Turn to page 333

"Listen Kera. I like you, but I'll be damned if I'm going to put on a blindfold in a dark alley downtown at 12:30 a.m. and be led into some sort of unknown hardcore techno club that sits secretly behind a steel door. You're askin' quite a bit here."

"Have it your way, then" she says disappointed. You feel a little bad and sense your opportunity to have sex with her is slipping away rapidly. Kera tucks the blindfold back down her bosom and hammers on the door with her fist.

After a moment, the door opens to reveal a complete and utter blackness you haven't seen since the time you visited the Fairy Caves when you were twelve and that fuckin' tour guide turned out all the lights to see "cave darkness". *Bitch! Scared the shit out of me is more like it.*

You survey the spectacle of a person who opened the door. The man (you're guessing) has long, jet black hair and white makeup covering his(?) face. He's sporting poorly applied bright red lipstick giving the impression that Helen Keller is his makeup consultant. His outfit consists of a floppy, lacey black top spilling over uncomfortably tight leather pants. As Kera walks by him, you can't help but notice the contrast between his dark gothic clothing and Kera's gorgeous white skin radiating beneath her blue dress, the last bit of sky at dusk before all sunlight is gone.

Music assaults your ears, drowning out everything around you as you enter the club. The rhythmic pounding of the song commandeers your heartbeat, and your body pulses to the dissonance. As SheMan, Master of the Underverse, closes the door behind you, the last rays of the single bulb outside catch Kera's perfect ass for one brief second before the two of you plunge into total darkness. You feel Kera's hand seek your own and she pulls you onward.

A few seconds later, Kera pulls a heavy black curtain away to reveal a seething mass of people thrashing wildly to German industrial music. Lights spiral and bounce over the waves of bodies crashing against each other. She looks at you and smiles before reaching down to pull her cute dress up over her head. Her unveiling reveals a tight leather bustier and short skirt that must have been concealed beneath her clothes this entire time. *What the fuck have I gotten myself into?* you think to yourself.

You take off your hoody since the place is sweltering. Without anywhere to put it, you drop it on the floor next to the wall, hoping against hope that you can find it again at the end of the night.

You follow Kera into the throng of people and she starts to lash out this way and that as if having a violent fit. The pounding music and heat mix with the booze from earlier to make you feel incredibly nauseous.

———————————

Go to the bathroom, puke and try to rally?
Turn to page 86

Try to find a way out of this freakshow.
Turn to page 43

"Ok, ok. You caught me," you say, flashing that winning smile of yours. "That's all I remember from high school Spanish. I was honestly trying to impress you."

"Really? That's all the Spanish you remember? I am thinking you might be a little slow, no?"

"No! Honestly, I'm pretty smart. I graduated with a bachelor's degree in Communications," you protest.

"Isn't that the American degree for people who just want to party at university?" Her broken English is not sounding so cute anymore.

"No, no. Not at all. I'm totally going into sports broadcasting as soon as I get my big break."

"Do you announce sporting events now?"

"Well no, not really. I mean, I announced a high school basketball game a few years back and… I mean, I'm totally going to look into announcing more games here once football season starts up."

"Uh huh. So, where do you work now?" Sofia asks.

You wince. *Dammit.* Hesitantly you say, "I work at a coffee house right now, but I'm planning on getting an internship at the local TV station someday soon. It's definitely going to happen. Just you wait and see." You can hear the desperation creeping into your voice.

"Soon?" You don't know how to respond and decide that Sofia is a real bitch.

"Hey listen, I'm gonna go find my friend. I think he just texted me. I'll, uh, catch you later."

"Bye bye, sport announcer guy." *Yup, she's a bitch.*

You leave her at the bar and start looking for Pete, hoping that he didn't take your suggestion to leave seriously. After fifteen minutes of looking, you come to the conclusion that *yup, he did. Well, shit.*

You call a taxi and head home feeling belittled and kinda drunk.

The End

You steal a glance to witness one of them direct the others to where Loretta is sitting. You start to panic, but Loretta puts her hand on your arm to calm you. When they get to your table, one of them roughly grabs Loretta by the back of her dress and pulls her to her feet.

She screams dramatically, "Get your hands off me!", shrieking above the ambient noise. She flails her arms pathetically against her assailant's chest, obviously hamming up the performance for the benefit of all eyes now trained on her.

You have no idea what she's trying to pull, but she's going to get herself killed. You want to stand up to help but are paralyzed with fear. You look around, gauging what effect this is having on the crowd. The surrounding patrons are clearly none too happy to have their night interrupted, and the poet onstage stops his reading. Silence falls over the club.

Struggling against her captors, Loretta looks back at you, importuning you with her eyes to do something. You swallow hard. *Ok, now or never.* You summon your courage, stand up and scream "It's me you want, you pig fuckers!"

You whip off your wig, and stand there in your dress, silhouetted by the light of the stage behind you. The country boy lets go of Loretta who crumples like a wilted flower to the floor with an extremely feminine gasp. You feel your adrenaline rising as well as a mounting desire to run like hell.

"Well, I'll be. Lookie 'ere boys, we gots ourselves a faggot wannin' to tussle." This statement obviously doesn't sit well among the patrons, and you can feel the energy in the club rising.

"I'm sorry. What'd ya say, you tractor-ridin' fuck?!" you scream back at them, egging them on.

A different hick answers you, gesturing with his bat. "Ya'll best be shutin' up fag if ya know wut's good for ya! I'm fixin' to shove this wooden bat so far up your ass no man will ever be able to satisfy your faggotty love hole."

Two tables away a large man in an ill-fitting, pink polka-dotted dress stands up. "Hey, I don't know what you have against this guy, but you can't talk like that in here."

"Who says I can't, faggot? You?"

"How about me?" answers another man in the club, standing up, rising tall with his blonde beehive hairdo perched precariously on his head.

"Or me?" chimes in a deep-voiced, overweight man, who stands up dressed as a very gay Marlon Brando from "The Wild One". In a mishmash chorus, most of the patrons proceed to join in, menacingly rising to their feet, issuing an answer to the challenge thrown down.

The good 'ol boys say nothing and merely move closer together to defend one another. Again silence.

Finally, one lone voice breaks the stillness of the room. "I think you fellas need to leave. You're not welcome here."

"Not without Mr. LoveCockLongTime over there. His faggot ass has to be taught a lesson."

"That's it!" you hear from somewhere and all hell breaks loose. In these close quarters the wooden bats are relatively useless. Within minutes, all four are set upon with an unholy fury of fists and feet– helpless against countless hours spent at the gym perfecting the perfect male body.

Loretta bursts from the melee, heading straight for you. "Good job, sweetie! You played along wonderfully! Let's get the hell outta here!"

You cast off the binding shoes from your feet. Sparing no time, you make for the fire exit pointed out by Loretta. As you make your way to safety, you thank God for the unwavering mutual support of the citizens of the gayborhood.

Leaving the club, you know you'll always remember your adventures with Loretta the Drag Queen.

The End

Loretta jerks the wheel down. The car careens right, loses traction and then spins wildly out of control. The approaching car slams on its brakes, smoke billows from the wheel wells, but it's too late. You side-swipe the approaching car– HARD.

The two cars collide in a dramatic crunch of metal and glass and you are thrown like a rag doll against your seat belt, you head cracking against your shoulder. You're instantly disoriented, shaken up by the accident. You close your eyes and try to clear your head.

Upon opening your eyes, you look over at Loretta and are startled to see that her luscious blonde hair was just a wig, now lying on the floor at her feet. You reach over to grab her shoulder and pull her gently toward you off the wreckage of the driver's side window.

"Loretta? Are you ok? Are you hurt?" No response. You reach up and gently turn her chin toward you. To your horror, blood covers the side of her face, down her neck and into her dress. You inspect her closer. Blood mats down her close-cut brown hair from a sizable chunk of glass embedded in her head. You panic.

"Loretta? Loretta! Can you hear me!" *Fuck.* She's out cold and badly needs a doctor. You take note of the rest of her, looking for other injuries. You notice that her breasts are out of place, skewed unnaturally. With a delicate touch, you reach over to touch one of them, wondering what injury could possibly have offset her chest.

Unfortunately, your question is forever left unanswered. Your assessment of Loretta's condition has distracted you from the fact that one of the pickup trucks is barreling toward you. It t-bones you on your side of the car, killing you instantly. You're dead.

The End

"That's so funny you should ask that! I just turned thirty last week!" you lie. A dark cloud passes over Foxy's face.

"Did you say you just turned thirty?"

"Yup. Last Wednesday. I went out with some of my buds. We went out drinking– got all fucked up. It was a blast! I wish I had known you then," you lie again, especially there at the end.

"Stay right here. I'll be right back." Foxy says cautiously and drawn out, as if you might go somewhere.

"Uh… sure. I'll just eat up some more of this jello stuff you made." Frowning, Foxy leaves the room. You're a little confused why her mood changed so drastically, but hey, maybe Aunt Flo's in town.

You hear some rustling around in the kitchen– a few muffled swear words followed by the crash of a number of pans being pulled from the cabinet.

"Everything ok in there?" you shout in after her.

"It's fine. It's all just fine. Just…keep eating. Don't leave. I'll be right there."

Don't leave? What the hell is that all about? Suddenly you hear an *Ah-HAH!* come from the kitchen followed by a soft metallic click and another harder metallic click. You put your plate down and turn toward the kitchen, fully curious what's going on. It's only moments until your question is answered.

Extremely serious, Foxy steps out from the kitchen, pointing what looks to be a pistol at you. *Oh God,* you sigh, *what the hell is she doing now? Please tell me that the Prom Queen of Looneyville isn't going mix role playing into sex tonight.*

"You need to go to the Carousel." Foxy says in a deadpan voice. You close your eyes in response and sigh deeply, preparing yourself as if dealing with the mentally ill.

"Listen honey, I'm tired and horny and I'll be honest, I really either want to have sex or just leave. I'm sorry to be so direct, but I think you're one of those people that don't deal well with inferences and subtle cues. You have a very nice

1970's enclave here, and were it another night, I'd be down with some Starsky and Hutch role playing or whatever the fuck it is that you are trying to do. But not tonight. Not tonight."

"Listen Runner, you have to go to the Carousel. It's the Law. You must be renewed! As a Sandman, it's my job to take Runners like you back to the Carousel."

"Foxy, I am not going to some damn carnival! It's fucking late, and I'm in no mood to ride the carousel, the Tilt-A-Whirl or the goddamn Ferris Wheel. Now put down your toy gun and get over here and let me kiss you," your voice echoing your rising ire.

"I'm sorry. If you're unwilling to go to the Carousel, I must assume you are a Runner and Runners must be terminated!" Before you can get out a protest, Foxy aims the gun and you and pulls the trigger. Nothing happens.

Ha ha, you think to yourself. *Very funny.* You stand up and move toward Foxy, tired of her horseplay. As you move toward her, you look in her eyes, a little nervous what you might find. *Is she kidding about all this or indeed truly fucking crazy?*

Lighten the mood with a joke.
Turn to page 186

Run like Hell.
Turn to page 223

"Sanctuary doesn't exist! It doesn't exist! THERE IS NO FUCKING SANCTUARY!!" you scream through tears brought on by your impending death.

Foxy stops and freezes. Her chin suddenly tilts down, almost mechanically. Her eyes widen and glaze over.

"Input does not program. You broke city seals and went outside! Input contrary. Unacceptable! Unacceptable!" Her arm rigidly holds the gun aimed squarely at you while she keeps repeating the word "Unacceptable" louder and louder, growing more aggravated with each repetition.

Now you REALLY don't know what to think. *What the hell is going on here?!* You start to move slightly to the side so the gun is no longer aimed directly at your face. To your surprise, the gun remains stationary, aimed where you had lain. You manage to roll over completely, well out of the path of the bullet.

Foxy, still screaming, jerks her head stiffly from side to side. You prop yourself up at the porch railing and cautiously pull out your cell phone, dialing 911 without even looking at the keypad. *God knows what she could do next.*

"Unacceptable! Unaccept..." Foxy lowers her arm and crumples to the porch, her eyes wide open and staring straight ahead. *Uh...*

You bring your phone slowly up to your face, hearing the operator saying something on the other end, coming though all tinny and incomprehensible. Staring all the while at the prone figure in front of you, you say one word quietly into the receiver... "Help." You then lower the phone, leaving it open and connected, knowing that the 911 operator will trace the call using your phone's built in GPS and send a squad car your way. Sometimes less is more– especially when explaining situations involving loonies.

You lean back against the railing and take off your tie as quietly as possible. Using it as a tourniquet to stanch the bleeding in your leg, you listen to the approaching sirens already wailing in the distance.

The End

"Whoa whoa whoa. Settle down there, Kitty," you quickly say, using your free hand to politely brush her away before she discovers the secret your other hand is keeping down.

"What's the problem?" Kitty asks.

"Uh…nothing. Nothing really. I…uh…ooooooh, it's my stomach. I just don't feel well to be honest, and I think I'm going to go. I'll just find Thad and, well, go I guess. I'm really sorry." You grimace in mock pain and throw in a grunt for good measure. You promptly stand up. "Ok. I'll see ya later."

"Oh. Ok. Yeah. I'll call you. What's your number?"

In anticipation of this question, you've already started moving away. You grimace again and then politely wave back at her, pretending to be out of hearing range. You rapidly turn your back so she can't ask any more questions. WHEW! You breathe an enormous sigh of relief.

You scan the club's dance floor to find Thad and Round Two. You instantly spot them near the speakers at the far end of the dance floor, the BubbleGum Avenger sticking out in the crowd like a sore thumb. You circle around to be out of sight of Kitty and then step up to the pulsating, illuminated surface. You straighten your tie and break out the swagger once again as you make your way toward them. Smooth as silk, you weave your way through the dance floor to where the new couple is dancing. They are doing some sort of coordinated dance thing which is way out of your ability range, so you just stand nearby, nodding your head to the beat, all the while attempting to make eye contact with Thad.

After a frustratingly long time, he finally looks your way and sees you. You flick your head to suggest that he should come over and talk. He politely excuses himself and maneuvers over.

"What's up?" Thad asks loudly over the thumping music.

"CatChick was a no-go. How's Pinky over there?"

You enter Kitty's bedroom as she is depositing Chairman Meow on the bed. He promptly lies down on the thick comforter and puts his head down on his outstretched front paws. Kitty reaches around and unzips a hidden zipper in the back of her leopard skin pants. They tumble to the floor, revealing the slightest of g-strings beneath, threading its way up her shapely ass.

"Lay down," Kitty commands you. You obey and sit on the edge of the bed, reclining back on to your elbows.

"Huh uh. Flip over." You smile and roll onto your stomach. You scoot yourself forward a little so that only your feet are hanging off the bed. You cross your arms and lay your head down, facing away from Kitty. You close your eyes, wondering what she has in mind.

The bed creaks and you can feel Kitty getting up on the bed next to you. You hear some movement and then feel her straddle you over your ass, her smooth, strong legs rubbing sensuously against your hips. She starts off by lightly dragging one hand slowly down the center of your back. Your whole body tingles at her touch. With every movement she makes atop of you, it electrifies your senses as it pushes and strokes the General against the bed.

"Ready?" Kitty asks.

"Oh yeah. I'm ready."

A soft, furry touch with a leathery center strokes your back. It's a unique feeling akin to being caressed by a feather but even more velvety and supple. It's very erotic, sending a quiver through your body. After a few strokes, Kitty starts making sexy, angry cat noises. It's 'Kitty Porn' you think to yourself and chuckle.

Then a piercing pain bursts through your pleasant erotic haze, and you feel sharp needle-like objects rake down your back. It's breaking the skin, and you scream out in pain and surprise.

"What the fuck!" you yell and twist your head back to see what exactly is going on. Out of the corner of your vision, you make out that Kitty is holding Chairman Meow, a limp dishrag of a cat, over your back with her hands on the pads of his paws, forcing his claws out. The bitch is using the cat on your back as foreplay!

_____

Freak out!
Turn to page 148

Tell her to lose the cat.
Turn to page 283

You roll to the side, causing Kitty to lose her balance and fling Chairman Meow off the bed as she reaches down to catch herself.

"Wait! What are you doing?" Kitty screams out.

"I'm getting the fuck out of here is what I'm doing. You are a crazy cat lady through and through, and there is no way in hell I'm going to spend another minute being felt up by your freakin' cat! That's it! I'm done." You stand up and walk determinedly through the door, down the hall to your pile of clothes. You toss your shirt on quickly, not bothering to button it, and slip your still-knotted tie over your head.

"But... but... but. I mean, we haven't had sex yet. You can't leave! I'll lock out all my roommates, I promise." Kitty pleads while walking towards you, practically naked, holding and stroking the big orange tabby.

You've donned your socks and start to the front door, trying to put your pants on while still holding your shoes. It's not going very well.

"Listen, you raked my goddamn back with a cat SEXUALLY! There's something wrong wi–"

You are unable to finish your sentence because you accidentally step on your half-raised pant leg, and it pulls you forward into the low hung sand mobile. "Oh fuck!" you yell as you throw out your shoe-bound hand in an effort to push the mobile out of the way while you careen toward it. One of the baubles skates deftly by and hits you square in the face against your lips, part of it breaking off into your half opened mouth. You plummet awkwardly to the floor, one hand resolutely holding your pants partially up and the other still holding both shoes firmly by their backs. As such, you have no way to catch yourself, so you slam down onto your shoulder. Pain shoots through your arm.

You close your mouth, ready to spit out the grit within, when you notice that what you taste is not sand. It's...it's...OH FUCK! It's kitty litter! That's a swinging mobile of hardened cat shit! The "box" she took it from was the cats' litter box. You spit it out frantically, and keep spitting with as much saliva as you can muster.

"Oh, my treasure box mobile! What have you done?! You've destroyed it!" Kitty shrieks out. You refuse to answer on account of your more pressing need to spit as much as possible.

You drop your shoes for a second to jerk your pants up then grab them and stand up. You don't even hesitate to button your pants as you reach for the front door and fling it open. You run out, spilling out of your clothes, disregarding your state of undress for the simple need to get as far away as fucking possible from the 'House of Pussy'.

Holding your pants up with one hand while you run, you make it about a block before you stop. You are panting heavily, the taste of kitty litter still lingering on your tongue. You turn and feverishly seek for a garden hose at the houses around you. Finding one sitting in the front yard two doors down, you rush toward it, fling your shoes to the ground, and turn on the water full blast.

The water rushes out, initially tepid and tasting like vinyl. You let it course over your tongue for a full minute before shooting it into your mouth, swishing and spitting a few times over. Satisfied that the poo pellets are finally washed out, you turn the hose off, and see to redressing.

After you have both shirt and pants buttoned, you take off your soggy socks and stuff them into your shoes. Both are soaked from your desperate mouth washing. You pull out your cell, thanking God it's still in your pocket, and call up Thad.

"Dude, I need you to come pick me up. Holy shit, have I got a story for you!"

The End

"Ok. I guess you can drive. Mind bringing me back here tomorrow morning to get my car?"

She just smiles at what you are suggesting but says nothing. The two of you leave for the parking lot. Only a few cars populate the area, and the car Kera heads toward is by far and above the nicest of the bunch.

"Holy shit, nice wheels!" you exclaim, sinking into the plush leather seats of her white Lexus.

"Oh, this ride's just getting started," she says with a broad smile on her lips and furtively winks at you.

The two of you drive toward the city. You find it's a bit hard to focus on the road with your eyes constantly drifting off center. God, maybe you have had a lot to drink.

"Hey, you ok to drive?" you ask, a little wary now that you recognize how drunk you are.

"Oh yeah. No worries. My drinks weren't that strong, my little drunkie monkey. I like them to have only a small splash of vodka in them."

"Right on. Well I gotta say, I'm pretty shitfaced," you inform her, slightly swaying in your seat, looking a bit like Joe Cocker. She giggles.

After a while, (you really have no idea how long) you realize you're downtown in an area of the city you've never seen. Kera pulls over and parks the car between two others on the street.

"We're here!"

"Where?" you ask incredulously. "There's nothing open here. I mean, I may be drunk, but the whole street is dark from where I'm sitting."

"Oh silly. It's just a little hard to see. I'll show you. Come on, let's go." Kera gets out of the car and you reluctantly follow.

The street is lit only by a few widely spaced streetlights leaving most of it in darkness. The two of you walk halfway down the block and Kera stops in front of an alleyway. She grabs your hand and starts down the dark alley.

"Where the fuck are we going? You're not going to kill me are you?" you joke halfheartedly.

"Sheeesh. Have a little faith. It'll be fun, you'll see. I promise."

About a hundred feet down the alley, Kera stops before a non-descript door, illuminated by a single bulb on the wall. The door is made of rusty steel covered in flaking white paint. Large bolts dot the surface like a page of Braille, almost like something you'd see on a submarine. You can hear the muffled sounds of industrial music pounding from behind the door, as if trying to break free of its imprisonment. You definitely feel a bit scared now but honestly, what could happen? Kera seems very nice and you kinda need her to get home.

"So… I want to surprise you," Kera says animatedly. She magically pulls out a thin strip of black fabric from her bra and holds it between her hands. "I want to blindfold you. It'll be fun, a real surprise. I promise it'll blow your mind!"

"It's blowing my mind right now!" you exclaim.

Trust Kera and put on the blindfold.
Turn to page 152

Fuck that. I want to see what I'm getting in to.
Turn to page 131

"Ok, I'm game. Go ahead and blindfold me," you say with reluctance.

Kera smiles and walks behind you with the blindfold. She gently loops it around your head. You hold it in place with your hands as she ties it in the back. Snug but not uncomfortable, the blindfold shuts out the light completely, especially in the darkened alley.

You hear Kera rap loudly on the massive steel door and grinding metal hinges screech as the door opens. Kera grabs your hand and leads you inside. Deafening music floods your ears as you draw deeper into the belly of the club. You sniff. The air is sweet and a bit salty and you can feel the heavy humidity in the air. Kera squeezes your hand in reassurance as you slowly proceed in, shuffling your feet, afraid you might trip over something.

You brush by something that feels kinda rubbery and warm and you pull back your hand quickly. *What the hell was that?*

You stop and feel the presence of someone near your head. Kera's voice rises above the music as she yells into your ear.

"Now, don't panic. I want you to hold out your hands."

You yell back, unsure if she can hear. "It's really hot in here. I'd like to take off my hoody first, if that's ok?"

You feel an accepting pat on your back, so you remove your sweatshirt, the blindfold not moving despite your intent that it might. Kera takes your superfluous garment while you obey her request. You extend your wrists, feeling a soft furry bracelet encircle one and then the other. The next thing you feel is Kera's hands at the back of your head, untying the blindfold.

As the blindfold comes off, you are hardly prepared for what greets your eyes. The pounding music is accompanied by red and orange lights spiraling around the club, illuminating some of the most alarming things you've ever seen.

All around you, people are dressed in black leather and latex, some with their faces hidden behind masks that only show their eyes and a small round hole for their mouth. There are ball gags binding the mouths of some, while others are bound completely in tethers, some anchored to their body by enormous, painful-looking piercings. All around you, people are doing things you've only heard about– candle wax dripping on naked bodies, whips in play leaving red welts upon exposed asses in specially designed pants. Both men and women, everywhere, enacting fetishes you never thought people really did.

You turn to look in horror at Kera. This is NOT what you had in mind at all. Kera just stands there, smiling broadly, an island of purity in this ocean of sin, her pale skin pushing back against the darkness.

With a flourish, Kera reaches down and pulls her dress up over her head exposing a sleeveless liquid latex suit underneath that joins the top of her boots. Her extremely low top shows off her gorgeous cleavage. After this momentarily stunning reveal, the reality strikes you again that you're in an S & M fetish dungeon.

You look down at your hands and notice that the furry bands are indeed handcuffs linked by a light aluminum chain. *Oh shit.*

Kera flicks her eyebrows up in a playful manner as she smiles at you. She approaches you and places her hands on your hips. You're not quite sure what she's going to do until she rapidly descends in front of you, pulling your pants to your ankles.

Her hands trail sensuously up your legs as she slowly rises in front of you. You're simultaneously getting aroused by her seductive outfit and aggressive undressing, but certainly turned off by the modern day Sodom and Gomorrah all around.

Now eyelevel, Kera grabs your shirt, her hands resting squarely on your pecs. With pinpoint precision, her fingers expertly find your nipples and give them a harsh tweak. You grimace but have definitely had worse growing up. Then, unexpectedly, with more strength than you would have given her, she tears your shirt off leaving you chained and mostly naked in a room full of the same.

―――――――――――――

Do you protest to Kera and tell her you want to leave?
Turn to page 69

Bring it on!
Turn to page 170

"Dude, I know you're all hot on this strip club idea but honestly, I gotta say that nobody ever gets lucky at a titty bar. It's all show and no touch. How 'bout we check out a dance club downtown instead? Chicks love to dance. I gotta think our luck would be much better there for hooking up purposes."

"Yeah, I guess," Kevin responds, a little crestfallen that you're not on board with his titty bar idea.

"Listen, I'll be over in an hour. Think you'll be ready by then?

"Sure, no problem. See ya in a few." Kevin hangs up.

An hour later you pull up in front of Kevin's. A signaling honk from the street brings him out. He's dressed well in a dark black suit with a trim cut to show off his chiseled physique. Now excited for the night, Kevin talks animatedly about all the pussy he's gonna bag and ass he's gonna tap. It's the standard, pre-night pep talk that he gives every time you guys go out and, as usual, lasts for most of the car ride.

It's not long before the two of you are downtown and visiting a favorite pickup joint. It's a happening spot, high on the radar for hot, single chicks who are out for a night dancing. The music pulsates around you. Colored lights scatter over throngs of gorgeous ladies on the dance floor, illuminating their lithe bodies briefly before cascading over the crowd to highlight others.

"Dude, you gotta check out that brunette dancing over there!" you say and point her out to Kevin. She's wearing a tight black number cut high to show off her marvelous legs.

"Oh shit yeah dude. You need to hit that. How about I buy us some drinks to get the party rollin'? What do you want?"

You are about to respond when you remember that Kevin's tastes tend toward top-shelf liquor. If he buys this round, you'll be on the hook for an expensive next round.

"No, I'm sorry. I just want to turn in. Here's my number though." You scribble down a series of random digits on the back of a receipt from your wallet and hand it to her. "Call me later and we'll hang out. Ok? Nice meeting you, Margaret," you lie.

You turn and walk toward your house. A few seconds later, you hear the door of the cab close and the drone of the motor fade in the distance. You unlock your front door.

"Sure I can't have just one little drink?"

What the fuck! You turn around to find Margaret standing on the sidewalk behind you. Her coat is open and her marvelous breasts are showcased by the lacework on her dress. Moonlight plays off her dark hair. She's really lovely, a dark angel standing in front of your home.

You sigh deeply. "Sure. What the fuck ever. Come in." You look at your watch. It's fuckin' late and you really don't want to have a drink with Mental Margie. Margaret scurries up the sidewalk and comes inside. You close the door behind her.

"Listen. I honestly don't want to drink with you. I'm beat. I've had a helluva day and I just want to go to bed, ok? If you want a drink, the booze is over there and there's beer in the fridge. Help yourself to whatever. And shit, if you wanna crash here, there's the couch. Now, I'm going to bed. Goodnight."

You feel a little bad being so abrupt with her, but this is your house goddammit and she just needs to get over herself. You shower and climb into bed. You lie there for a second, listening in the dark for sounds of what Margaret might be up to. It's pretty quiet out in the living room, so maybe the whack-o has crashed out on the couch. You sigh a deep, tired sigh. *Hopefully she won't steal all our DVDs,* you think as you drift off to sleep.

At some point during the night, you hear a loud crash that jolts you awake. *What the hell is that bitch up to?!* You climb out of bed wearing only your boxers and open the door to the hallway. It's dark. You step out and head down to the living room, trying to discern what must have happened. You're not happy.

"Jesus Christ, Margaret! What the hell are you doing? You're waking up the whole goddamn house!" you yell.

Suddenly, without warning, an enormous man fills the hallway in front of you. You stop, unsure if what you're seeing is real. *Am I dreaming?* you wonder.

"Where the fuck is the broad?" the stranger asks, a long angular form jutting from his arm, both silhouetted in the dark.

"Who the fu-" is all you get out before his shotgun goes off, carving a massive hole in your chest.

Moral of the story: *Never answer a question with another question. It annoys people.*

The End

she's doing MORSE CODE WITH HER VAGINA!! You nod to show her you understand what she's doing.

G...U...N.../...U...N...D...E...R.../...B...E...D

Her eyes look inquisitively up at you. You nod again, almost imperceptibly, and slowly reach over the side to the floor. You brush your hand underneath the bed. Your fingers meet the cold touch of steel. *How the hell did that get there?* you wonder. You sure as hell don't own a gun. Moreover, you haven't even shot one since you were up at your uncle's farm eight years ago. *What the fuck is happening here?*

You clutch the gun and roll off Margaret. Confused, you show it to her as if to say, "What the hell is this doing under my bed and why the fuck am I being so quiet?!" Margaret, instead of answering your unspoken question, flicks her head up toward the window. Slowly, she crouches on the bed and reaches up to it. It opens with a small squeak that in the stillness of the house seems like the scream of a toddler.

Margaret pauses for an instant to listen to the ringing silence of the house. You sure as shit don't hear anything. A bit irate with this whole dramatic production, you begin to say something when suddenly you hear footsteps clomping around the house. Margaret looks at you as if to say, "See Jackass! I told you someone was here!"

It scares the hell out of you to have strangers in your home. You feel violated. Your hand with the gun is shaking, making the likelihood of actually hitting anything unlikely.

Margaret crawls out first, her gorgeous ass moving hypn– *focus, goddammit! Focus!* you tell yourself. You stand on the bed, placing the gun on the windowsill. The sound of heavy footsteps on the wooden floor outside your door grows louder.

"They're in here!" a rough voice calls out. You swiftly turn to see a thug dressed in a long overcoat open the door.

In a single motion, he casts open the right side of his trench and reaches into the dangling shoulder holster for his gun. Instinctively, you grab your weapon off the windowsill, whip it around and start firing wildly, hoping to God that maybe you'll hit him.

Bang! Bang! Bang! The shots ring out from the chamber in quick succession until the clip is empty and the gun clicks in protest. You're out. Without wasting a second, and without seeing if you actually hit anything, you hunker down and take a big bounce on the bed. You sail out the window, tossing the gun before you. You tuck your chin and try to emulate doing a flip at the pool so that you will land on the ground feet first.

However, given the fact that you've never actually completed a flip at the pool, your attempt skews into a back flop as it always does. You knock the wind out of yourself when you hit the ground.

Mysterious Margaret retrieves the gun and checks the clip to see how many bullets remain. Seeing that you've emptied it, Margaret scowls and yells for you to get up off your ass. She then turns and flees.

Your back in excruciating pain, you roll over and stand up. Hand on your back like an old man, you run with a limping gait. Not more than ten steps taken, you hear gunshots again in the house. *Fuck!* You turn to look back. *Those fuckers must have shot Thad!! What the hell have I gotten myself into?*

You begin to sob as you run away, frightened and unsure what events have been set in motion around you.

The End

You enter the club, not sure what to expect. What you find is a time capsule of one of the greatest nightclub eras the U.S. has ever known.

The first thing you notice upon entering the club is the technicolor floor composed of multicolored carpet squares. There is no rhyme or reason to the pattern suggesting, at least to you, that the carpet installers were clearly blind. The focus of the club is a raised stage that lights up in various geometric patterns– sometimes pulsating in concentric squares, other times flashing in outwardly expanding diamonds. The stage is completely full of dancers, funkin' their bodies to the riffs that fill the hazy air. Streams of light pierce the thick atmosphere from the swirling disco ball overhead. Various high tables are scattered surrounding the dance floor for the standing crowd. At the club's periphery are white leather couches for patrons to cuddle. The walls are covered in posters bearing the essence of the club's namesake– films like *Sweet Sweetback's Baadasssss Song*, *They Call Me MISTER Tibbs!*, *Blacula, and Dolemite.*

You look at Thad and nod approvingly. Overtop of the pounding slapped bass, you scream to Thad, "Let's head over to the bar!" Thad agrees wordlessly by smiling and following you.

The bar is a brilliant, mirrored affair staffed by a man who bears a striking resemblance to Redd Foxx. You definitely admire the club owner's attention to detail. You pick up the small, folded card on the bar that lists the specials of the night. Not surprisingly, many of them are classic names in malt liquor: Schlitz, Olde English, and Colt 45. Others are classic brews of the era: Strohs, Schaefer, PBR. You order up a Colt 45 and Thad gets a PBR. You click your thick glasses together and each slam down at least half of your beer, a jump of liquid courage to get the night going.

You place your glass back on the bar and scope the happenin' honeys at the high tables. You mark two of 'em, both smoking Virginia Slims, delicately inhaling from the lengthy cigarettes.

One is clad in a fabulous, pink metallic spandex jump suit with a low slung ruffled collar that showcases the inner curves of her well-shaped tits. Her only other adornments are a thin golden metal belt that matches a tight, golden choker. She is perched atop tall, golden platform shoes that barely poke out from the flared pink pant legs. Long, brown, wavy hair parted in the middle falls unflatteringly around her beautiful face.

Next to her stands a woman with short-cropped, feathered, blonde hair clad in what can be best described as a tight-fitting cat suit with matching leopard print neck scarf. Her chest is barely covered by a bikini-style top, tied in the middle with straps that hang down to her high-waisted, tight, leopard print pants which majestically flair out where they meet the floor. Her face is radiant with full lips colored to mirror the smoky treatment given to her eyes.

Both ladies are clearly well ingrained into the 1970's scene despite the fact they are probably in their mid-twenties. You wouldn't be surprised if they are high on blow, perhaps making your job of wooing them that much easier. Time to make your move!

Pickup the Disco Paratrooper.
Turn to page 325

Hit up the Lascivious Leopard Lady.
Turn to page 187

"Let's just say I'm in my late twenties and old enough to sex your foxy ass up."

"Whew. That's good."

Just then, the front door opens disrupting the calm of the dogs, sending them into another welcoming frenzy for the couple that enters. The woman has long, feathered brown hair and wears a skirt below a man's button down shirt, the two sides tied in the middle to make a bra. On the shirt is a large monogrammed 'L'. Holding her by the waist is a medium-sized man with a black, pencil mustache that matches his short, black, feathered hair. He's wearing a blue denim vest that has red striped shoulders overtop of a white t-shirt. One sleeve is rolled up around of a pack of smokes. His jeans show quite a bit of wear and it's clear that he probably makes a living in a blue collar profession.

Foxy introduces the visitors to you. "My roommate's home! I'd like you to meet Laverne and Schneider. Laverne and I go waaaaaay back. I helped her move from an abysmal basement apartment to get away from these two dirtbags who stalked her. It was horrible." You wave to the couple from the couch and smile politely.

"Hey listen Foxy, we're gonna go up to my room, if you need us. We don't want to bother you during Soul Train. Now, be good you two!" Laverne says with a wink. The two of them disappear, and you hear a door close down the hall.

It's not long after that you hear moaning and the squeaking of bed springs. That, coupled with the bad disco music playing equally loud on the TV, creates a scene of what you might expect to see in a bad 70's stag film. *Holy Jesus, Laverne is a screamer to boot! This is just all getting too surreal.*

Foxy, on the other hand, clearly finds it to be extremely erotic, and her hitherto suggestive dancing transforms dramatically into a striptease. Slowly, with her eyes locked to yours, she unclasps the golden belt at her waist and lets it fall with a metallic clank on the soft carpet underfoot. Then, with both arms, she reaches back and unzips the back of her spandex disco jumpsuit, the front peeling open to expose her beautiful, voluptuous breasts. The porno audio experience, coupled with this smokin' hot rack staring you square in the face, triggers all systems 'go' and your underwear gets uncomfortably too small. You smile, thinking to yourself, *FUCKING FINALLY!*

With a slow hand, Foxy peels down the pink spandex to reveal her panties underneath. Unfortunately, the 1970's were not a high point in lingerie, and the cut is not as flattering as you had hoped. *Who friggin' cares though!* You lean forward, ready for the finale.

Stepping from her jumpsuit with remarkable grace, Foxy stands in front of you, hands on her hips, her legs spread apart, wearing only her panties and golden broad-based heels. She pauses, letting your ravenous eyes eat up the woman you are about to fuck like an animal. After a moment, she reaches with one hand to caress the side of her face up into and through her wavy brown hair. Her head falls back as her chest extends toward you. Then, whipping her focus back to you, she brings her arm back down, stroking her breasts slowly on the way to her waist. She inserts one finger under the elastic waistband of her panties and stretches them down, the other side reluctantly following.

Holy shit!! You gasp involuntarily and sit back in shock. *Her love of the 70's didn't stop with her appreciation of the music.* Let's just say that where the rubber hits the road, the countryside reared up angrily and blocked the view. There must be a German village somewhere on her waist because there is a huge fucking black forest between her legs!

You stop to think for a second. You've come this far and she sure is smokin' hot, but in light of the flock of sheep she keeps in her panties, maybe it's time to reconsider. You're going to need a shepherd's crook to fuck this bitch!

You give a suggestive head nod to Kera, challenging her to do her worst. You're a man and can take whatever this crazy bitch can dish out. Make no mistake, this whole scene freaks your shit, but Kera is smokin' hot and if she's into the kinky stuff, whatever. *Who am I to judge?* you think to yourself.

Kera smiles snidely back at you and reaches over to grab a riding crop leaning against the wall. Her eyes narrow wickedly. Whooosh… **CRACK!** She brings the riding crop down hard on the side of your leg. It stings a helluva lot, but it's no kick in the nuts.

You grit your teeth and smile at Kera. *Do you worst, bitch. I dare you,* you tell her with your eyes. She comes in close. You can feel her breath as she rubs her chin up your chest to your face. She leans in, her lips brushing yours, making you ache for a kiss that never comes. Instead, Kera pushes you forcefully back. Your pants around your ankles bind your legs together and you fall backwards uncontrollably. You want to catch yourself with your hands but since you're handcuffed that just isn't an option. You topple.

This kinda pisses you off and you start to sit up, but the toe of Kera's boot sends you right back to the floor. She presses down on your chest with her foot, keeping you lying still in submission. You look up at her, her determined features so beautiful in the cascading lights overhead. *Fuck it,* you give in.

After that night with Kera you are sore for days, your body abused in ways never thought possible; but honestly, the end of the night made up for all of it. You and Kera made violent, passionate love three amazing times, the last time climaxing at dawn, the new day greeted with ecstatic screams.

A changed man, within weeks you have your own S & M body suit with matching ball gag. It's a whole new world.

The End

You flip open your phone and scroll down to Julie's number. *She'd be perfect,* you think. *A little overweight, kinda dorky– nothing special to look at. Just the girl!*

"Hey Julie? It's me. I'm callin' to see if ya wanna go out tonight and grab a drink?" you ask.

Julie responds enthusiastically. "Sure!"

You know that Julie isn't seeing anyone right now so best to be clear about tonight's purpose. "So listen, tonight's the night I'm diving back into the dating game and I wanna know if you're down with helping me score a winner."

A pause on the other line.

"Um… What do you have in mind?" she asks.

"Well, I'm all dolled up and I'm thinking of hitting a club downtown– maybe Hanger 69. You know, the 1960's one, with the waitresses dressed like airline stewardesses in cute little skirts and boxy hats? It's very hip right now. Very 'Mad Men'."

"Swanky." Another pause. "Oh what the hell, sure I'll help ya. How about this– I know you wanna drink tonight, so what say I drive?"

"Oh my God, you're a saint! You rock, Julie. I mean, seriously. You're the best."

"Ok there bud, settle down. I'll be by in forty-five minutes."

You hang up the phone and sure enough, forty-five minutes later, a car horn honks outside. You jet out, locking the door behind you and jump into Julie's car.

"Wow there Casanova! Pulling out all the stops, I see."

"Yeah," you smile slightly embarrassed. "And hey, you look good too."

Julie is wearing a nice, low-cut white sleeveless blouse with a camisole underneath to cover her generous breasts. Trousers with a wide cut leg round out her outfit. It's dressy, but not super feminine– just what you were hoping.

The two of you get to the club and pony up the twenty dollar cover charge. *Damn, this better be worth it. That's a mighty steep price just to get in.*

"You're right. I'm gonna do it! Watch me in action, Jules," you exclaim and stand up.

Julie sighs as you make you way to the bar. You order another drink, despite the fact you still have one at your table, and try to look casual. After a few minutes, you turn to the woman next to you. She's clothed in a well-fitted black dress with a décolletage that showcases her stunning bosom. A string of pearls sits closely around her neck. You break the ice.

"Hey, what's going on?"

"Nothing." she responds apathetically, not even really looking at you.

"Right on." Silence. That's all you get. *Damn, I shouldn't have drunk so much,* you think. *I'm off my game!* "Uh... so, what do you do for a living?" *Oh my God, this is getting bad.*

She turns to you and addresses you in a matter-of-fact tone. "Listen bud. I appreciate you trying to make conversation with me, but I'm here with some friends. Besides, your date is looking pretty lonely back at your table."

"Oh yeah, uh, her. Yeah, I should get back to her. Nice talking with you... bitch." the latter comment made under your breath, but not completely so.

You leisurely meander through the bar area with your drink. *Ok, need to be more aggressive. That was pitiful,* you think to yourself. *Hello? What do we have here?*

Two tables in front of you sits a woman all by herself, only one glass on the table. That's a good sign, suggesting that she's not with anyone.

You saunter drunkenly to the table and immediately take a seat, not waiting for an invitation. She looks a little surprised but also mildly amused. *Ok,* you think, *time to be the aggressive male. Chicks dig an aggressive approach.*

"Hey baby, how'd you like me to ride that vag canal like a fuckin' gondolier?"

SLAP! You're stunned. "Fuck you creep! That's so gross!" She immediately gets up and storms away.

You sit there, the side of your face pulsating a little where she hit you. It's not too bad as most of the pain is dulled by the booze. *Shit, strike two.*

For the next couple hours, you make your way around Hanger 69. You try dancing a bit, furtively working your way into the many cliques of girls dancing together. By and large each group tolerates you for part of a song before slowly reforming to put you on the outside. One group seemed promising, allowing you to dance with them for a number of tunes. But as soon as the amusement of your drunken rendition of the Running Man and other 80's dances wore off, they too left you alone.

You make your way back to the bar, dejected and feeling like a big fat drunken loser. All you want to do is find Julie and get the hell out of here.

Julie, you discover, is up at the bar drinking a beer.

You stroll over to her, head hung low. "Hey Jules. Let's go. This place blows. I'm ready to leave."

Julie looks up at you and then over at the woman sitting beside her– a beautiful woman in her 20's with long blonde hair wearing a business-like gray pantsuit.

"Um, I'd like to introduce you to Sandra," Julie says.

You unenthusiastically wave at Sandra muttering a "Hi", mostly just ready to get out of this hellhole.

"Hey, listen. Why don't you catch a cab home? I think I'm going to stay a while and hang out here with Sandra."

"What the hell! I thought you were going to drive! Dammit. What's so great about Sandra?" you retort, pissed off. "Sorry Sandra." you offhandedly apologize after the fact.

You lean in close to Julie, "She kinda looks like a dyke. Can we just go?" You know you're being an asshole but whatever, your night's been ruined.

"That's what drew me to her."

You pull back, the meaning of her statement sinking in. "What? You mean? Uh. I mean, you're a… <u>lesbian</u>?" you say incredulously.

Julie just winks and turns back to Sandra, animatedly apologizing for your behavior. You can't believe it but it sure as hell looks to be true. Julie is enraptured with Sandra and her conversation full of giggles and googley eyes proves it. You are quickly forgotten and storm away like a spoiled child.

At the door to the outside, you turn around one last time to see Julie and Sandra kissing passionately. *Dammit. She's gonna get lucky while I'm gonna get a taxi.*

Looks like your fun is going to consist of a bottle of lotion and the National Geographic channel at 3 a.m. watching a special about the promotion of breast feeding in Africa... again.

The End

You wrap your arms around Maggie's slender, white waist; and with a push of your foot, the two of you roll onto the floor. Your arms take the brunt of the small plunge with Maggie now underneath you.

"Oooooo, a man 'o lakes it ruf! Brin' it on, ya sexy bastard. Lat's see what ye got to give ol' Mags."

You smile coyly and move her legs to deliver yourself missionary style. As you're about to penetrate her, she stops you suddenly.

"WAIT a secund, boyyo! Yer not gonna be givin' me yer delivery like a pussy lad ar ya?"

"Well, I… I mean, we just met and I didn't want to go crazy or anything."

"Oh sweet Mother Mary! God in Haven, ya tro yerself at a man and he becombs a lattle girl. Don't ye know I was hintin' that I be wantin' somethin' ruf?"

"Oh, don't worry. I can be rough, honestly," you plead, the sexual air in the room rapidly fading.

Maggie reaches up and slaps you fiercely across the face. "Can ye tak that, pansy boy?"

Your temper flares aided by the testosterone flowing through you. *What the fuck?! It's one thing to call me a 'pansy' but you don't fuckin' slap me like a bitch!* You're pissed, but you've never hit a girl before. God knows you want to, but you can't retaliate– it's just not in you. Your pause gives you away.

"Git da fark off me, ya girl!" Maggie angrily pushes you off of her and starts to dress. You're torn. She's being a cunt, but goddammit she's hot. You begin to plead with her, telling her all the dirty things you can think of that you would be willing to do, but the moment has passed. You largely look now like a high school boy eager for his first attempt at sex. It's embarrassing and you know it, but you're thinking with your dick.

Maggie flips you the bird as she walks out of the house—her departing wisdom "to grow some bollocks" cut off by the slamming of the door. You sink down onto the couch, still naked and obviously not aroused anymore. *Fuck.*

The End

"Dude, you're totally right. It's one thing to have a one-night stand with a dumb chick, but unbalanced– that's where I draw the line," you say. "Any idea of an exit strategy?" you ask looking around, hoping that maybe the bathroom has a window you can shimmy out of. No luck.

Pete answers, "Well, I figure this place has to have a fire exit, right? The chicks are standing near the door, waiting for us. What say we make for the stage area instead and check for a fire exit there?"

"I'm down. Let's fly," you respond with hasty conviction.

Pete opens the bathroom door and peeks outside. He motions that the coast is clear. The two of you sneak your way to the opposite wall of the club from the front door. You try your best to blend in and act nonchalant. Unfortunately, it's a bit difficult given the fact that you are incredibly shitfaced and you're overacting by a great deal. At one point, you even start whistling, but thank God, Pete shuts you up quickly.

Sure enough, beside the stage is a fire exit. Pete crosses himself and says a little prayer that an alarm won't go off. He pushes the door handle. *Whew!* It opens quietly and the two of you scurry out into the night.

As it would happen, the door exits to the edge of a massive parking lot for an adjacent hotel. An ocean of cars greets you as the door slams shut. Both of you are completely turned around. You look to Pete for hope.

"Hey, uh, any clue where we parked?" you ask, praying that Pete, being a little more sober, might have a clue.

Pete pauses, casting his eyes around the seemingly infinite number of cars. "Nope."

"Shit. That sucks," you say crestfallen.

"Ok, how about this: I'll go look for the car cuz you're pretty hammered. You just sit tight here, and I'll be right back. Cool?"

"A-Ok, Capt'n!" You salute Pete drunkenly and then enthusiastically plop yourself down on the curb, relieved that

Pete is takin' charge. Pete heads off and is soon lost in the darkness.

You sit there on the curb, lost for time since Pete left. After a while you start thinking: Maybe you should go look for him. Or, maybe you should look for the car! Or, hmmmm… maybe you should just stay put.

_____

Stay put like Pete said.
Turn to page 304

Go look for Pete and the car.
Turn to page 330

You come screaming up to the dead end.

"Turn RIGHT!" you belt out as you grab the shitgrip above the door.

The Honda cuts the corner hard and the back end fishtails out into the adjacent lane, tires protesting vehemently. Close on your bumper now, the first pickup makes the turn almost in unison with you, fishtailing dramatically to continue its pursuit. However, the second truck catches the close edge of the pavement during the turn and flips. In a blink, the truck rolls across the road, side over side, debris cast out in a cloud of metal and dust. The truck's momentum carries it into the dirt beyond.

"Holy shit!" you exclaim. "He just flipped! The second truck just flipped! Did you see that? Jesus! That truck is all fucked up!" you excitedly tell Loretta.

The third truck makes the turn easily as its center of gravity is much lower than you would have guessed and it thrusts down the road toward you.

You reassess the odds. Two trucks now, probably four hicks– you're clearly not out of the woods yet. Streetlights stream by overhead in a slow strobe as you race toward downtown. At your rate of speed, you hit the downtown area in no time and are running red and green lights alike. It's all a blur. Thank God it's mostly deserted here so you ca–

"FUCK! CAR!" you scream as you're about to enter the intersection ahead of you. Loretta screams and lets go of the steering wheel in response. You grab the wheel as a late model Caddy enters the intersection to your right.

Jerk the wheel down!
Turn to page 59

Jerk the wheel up!
Turn to page 184

"Go! Go! Go!" you scream. Loretta drops into a lower gear and punches the accelerator to the floor, sending the tach needle spinning toward the red. The Honda jumps forward with a temporary surge of power. The other driver blares his horn which grows exponentially louder as you both approach the intersection. At the last second, the other car slams on its brakes, finally realizing you have no plans to stop. Both you and Loretta scream like little girls knowing that this may be your last moment on earth. By some miracle, you narrowly squeak by the other car.

Unfortunately, the truck close on your tail doesn't.

The opposing car slams full on into the truck, t-boning it, pushing it violently through the intersection. You turn to look at the accident over your shoulder, glad to reduce your pursuers by one but sorry for the other driver whose night just got ruined. The other two trucks continue past the accident, even more hell bent on catching you now.

"Alright Loretta, we're coming up to a neighborhood that's one step shy of being a labyrinth. In two blocks, you're going to turn right, K?"

The two blocks come quickly and with a squeal of her tires, Loretta makes a ninety degree turn into the covenant protected neighborhood.

"This will work, trust me," you reiterate. "I know this place like the back of my hand. See, just about every street in this godforsaken area has the same basic name– Gibbons Street, Gibbons Court, Gibbons Road– you get the idea. Once you're in, it's a bitch to get out. So step one: Let's get our friends back there a little lost. Here's how I want you to play it." You begin to tell Loretta a complex series of turns designed to bury you deep in the neighborhood.

Getting lost is going to be the easy part. Now the question is for step two: should we hide or try to lose them somewhere along the way?

Hide.
Turn to page 39

Lose 'em.
Turn to page 338

She's GOT to be kidding about all this. No one is honestly this crazy.

"How about we go to the carnival first thing in the morning? I promise we'll go." You smile at her. "Although I gotta be honest, riding those plastic horses kills my nuts. That damn plastic seam on the top pinches my ball sack!" You laugh lightly at your joke, attempting to suggest that it's time to stop playing around. Foxy does not laugh and examines the gun in earnest to discover why it didn't fire.

Suddenly her eyes open wide in discovery, and she pushes in a button on the side of the gun. *Holy shit. That was the safety! That's why the gun didn't fire!*

You throw up your hands in surrender and start to back away slowly from this fucking nutjob, but before you can even get two steps, Foxy trains the gun at your chest and fires.

In response, the gun recoils violently in her hands. Your ears deafen from the blast in the close quarters of the room. Immediately, you feel very lightheaded and an intense shock racks your body. It's then you realize you've been shot. In fact, that's the last realization you ever have. You're dead.

The End

You saunter over to the ladies, your swagger turned up to FULL, and connect with the eyes of CatWoman. You toss her a sly grin as you approach.

"Shiiiit baby! I ain't no rah rah silver bullet! This pinkpolo'd mofo knows a slammin' get 'em up beep beep when peeped." You wink at CatWoman. "Whatup, honey?"

Meanwhile, Thad quickly steps in and introduces himself to the Spandex Pinky, disarming her reproach from your complete dismissal of her presence. Catwoman just stares at you, obviously befuddled at what you said but a smile soon cracks her lips, and she starts laughing at your jive talkin'.

"That was really good," Catwoman says. "Where in <u>hell</u> did you pick that up?"

"Oh, I watched the movie *Airplane* probably about a billion times and then took a 'Dialects in Speech' class for my Communications major. The prof loved jive so much he made it a major focus of the curriculum. Who would've guessed it'd come in handy again!"

"Well right on! I can dig it."

"See, there ya go! Awww sooky sooky now. So, what do ya do for a living?" you ask.

"Promise not to laugh?"

"Well, I promise not to laugh out loud, how about that?"

"Hmmmm…. ok. I have an eBay business. I made edible underwear for Barbie dolls."

"You have to be shitting me! Can you actually sell enough to make a living? I mean, who the hell buys it?"

Catwoman smiles. "Fuck if I know. Probably pervs mostly, but hey, who am I to judge, ya know? I mold 'em out of Fruit Roll-Ups and decorate them with various food coloring inks. It's fun. I guess I'm just a frustrated fashion designer who found a strange niche and exploited it."

"Well ok then."

"Actually, I'm coming out with a bra line in the fall. It should be sweet, if you'll pardon the pun. Hell, maybe if that does well, I'll expand my business to real women.   But whatever. Enough about me, what do you do?"

"Well, as I said, I majored in Communications, but regrettably these days I mostly just communicate orders at the coffee bar where I work. It's a stop-gap job until I can get a real job."

"Which would be…"

"That's where we're in a little bit of a gray area, hence the three year duration of my current 'stop-gap' employment." Cutting your losses before the conversation paints you as a total loser, you quickly change topics, "So I never caught your name."

"Oh, silly me. My name is Katherine, but you can just call me 'Kitty'. The outfit should help you remember." Kitty smiles, her full lips parting to show beautiful, white teeth underneath.

"Yeah, I must say, I'm diggin' the threads! Turn around and lemme take it all in."

Kitty does as you requested– slowly turning 360 degrees, modeling her look by glancing upwards with her head slightly cocked to one side. You ogle her incredible body from the tight, perfectly wrapped ass to her narrow, toned torso exposed between her bikini-style top and leopard print pants. As she comes full circle, you note her well-endowed, yet perky breasts which are barely contained by the center-tied top. The dirty voice in your head begs you to set them free.

"Nice.   Very nice," you say, carefully controlling the sleaze factor in your voice.

"Well, right back at ya," Kitty says and smiles. "You're looking mighty fine in that suit and tie. I must admit I have a definite weakness for a well-dressed man." You grin smugly inside. *Ya damn right. I KNEW the suit would work!*

"Hey, I'm kinda hungry," Kitty says. "Wanna get some food? And p.s., I think your friend left with Foxy." You look over having completely forgotten Thad and notice that the two of them are gone. *Way to go bud! Helluva wingman! Free to pursue without hindrance.*

"Eh, he's fine. They're probably out dancing or something. So, whatcha hungry for? I'll go order it at the bar."

"Fries with Franch dressing, I think."

"You mean *Ranch* dressing?"

"No, Franch dressing," Kitty says, enunciating slowly. "It's a mixture of French and Ranch. Mmmmm… it's SO good. You dip the fries in it. Heavenly!"

"Uh, ok. If you say so." You go the bar and put in the order. The barkeep doesn't even blink when you order some "Franch" dressing on the side. *I guess it's not all that uncommon,* you think to yourself.

You head back to Kitty and in a few moments, a waitress brings out the fries with a small, red plastic cup of the magical 'Franch' dressing. Kitty, it appears, is ravenous and digs right in– dipping, biting, then double and triple dipping in the Franch before finishing each fry. She looks positively orgasmic the way she is savoring each and every bite.

"Wanna try some?" Kitty asks.

_____

Sure. Why the hell not.
Turn to page 102

No thanks, I'm good.
Turn to page 105

"Ok. Your loss," Kitty responds to your rejection of her fry peddling.

Kitty continues to eat her fries, truly savoring each one, slowing down only when the basket is nearly depleted. As if she's trying to torture you, she takes to dipping a fry into the French dressing and then licking the dripping sauce sensuously off the fry. Her tongue plays up and down the brown shaft before looking at you with sex in her eyes and re-dipping the fry.

On one hand, you're definitely getting aroused. On the other hand, this chick is licking fries and re-dipping them, which is kinda gross.

Her fry molestation continues for another round or two and then devolves into something much more disturbing. Rather than simply licking the fry, Kitty is now going down on it. Moaning, her eyes rolling back in her head, she deep throats the sliver of spud. When the last remaining fries are deflowered and finally swallowed because they've lost all dimensional stability, the show is over.

You're not quite sure what to say at this point. You're harder than shit, and it's a bit difficult to conceal. You do your best by holding yourself down with your pocketed hand. Despite that fact, reenacting bad porn using food is not quite an attribute you would choose in a woman. *I mean, she may have been kidding,* you tell yourself, *but she just didn't stop! If it were a joke, it went on way past the comfortable point. Ah, the eternal question, which head should do the thinking...*

"Sooooo..." Kitty starts slowly, "I was thinking. What say we move this feast back to the House of Pussy?" she asks, stretching out the final word, elongating it to sound more like *Pooooossy.* To further assert her request, Kitty puts her hand on your knee under the table and slowly starts caressing her way toward your ill-kept secret.

Oh God, should you go for it? Obviously the General thinks so! you note considering the tent threatening to spring up between your legs. *But what if there's more food porn, or she tries dripping hot wax on my nipples, or some other kind of freaky shit?* That could get kinda scary and weird.

Ya know, there is always the Spandex Pinky you *could* hit up instead.

Take a trip to the House of Pussy.
Turn to page 192

Abandon ship! Find Pinky the Paratrooper.
Turn to page 143

Eh, what the hell, you think to yourself. *Toughen the fuck up and be adventurous!* Besides, you reason, you'll leave the car for Thad and if the shit hits the fan, you can always call him to come get your ass.

"Let's head," you tell Kitty. "The House of Pussy shan't be kept waiting another minute! Oh, one quick thing, is it cool if we take your car? I need to leave mine for my housemate."

"Oh that's a purrrrrfect idea." Kitty makes a little clawing motion at you. *Uh...ok.*

Leaving the disco scene behind, you follow Kitty to her car– a beaten-up, reddish-orange Subaru with a white bumper sticker on it that says "Bast Lives!" with ankh symbol after it. The car sure as hell doesn't look all that safe. As you walk around to the passenger's side, you notice the left tail light is composed of peeling, red cellophane tape that poorly imitates the broken plastic that covered the light at one time. *Maybe taking Kitty's car isn't such a wise idea.*

You get in and the car sputters to life. You turn to put your seatbelt on, a wise move given the quality of your ride, but no matter how hard you jerk it, it refuses to budge.

"Oh sorry. I forgot to tell you the seatbelt is broken. But don't worry. I'm an <u>excellent</u> driver." *I doubt it, but here's hoping you are at least passable while I'm in the car.*

Kitty backs up and tears out of the parking lot at what seems like a hundred miles an hour. Ok, maybe it's not a hundred miles per hour, but with the mysterious rattling and occasional sound suggesting the loss of engine parts, it feels horribly unsafe. You grab the shitgrip idly and say a silent prayer that nothing happens like the goddamn car exploding or losing a tire or something.

After a harrowing, yet uneventful, twenty minutes or so you pull up in front of Kitty's small bungalow. The car backfires twice after wheezing out a final breath, and you're pretty damn sure you're going to have to call Thad in order to get home.

"Oh, it always does that," Kitty says, seemingly reading your mind and obvious concern on your face.

"Oh…uh…ok.   Seems like a dependable little car though," you lie.

"It gets me from point A to B and that's all I really need. Bast looks out for me. So come on in, the House of Pussy awaits!"

You follow Kitty into her home and immediately have to dodge a rather unique-looking mobile turning slowly in the foyer, hung way too low.   Multi-tiered, the mobile is composed of dangling bits of sandy ornaments affixed to clear nylon line.   These lines run to varnished twigs separating each gritty globe from the others. It runs a fine line between homemade and high end– a shabby chic piece of art that looks both modern and childish. You reach up to touch the gyrating objet d'art.

"Whoa whoa! Don't touch it! Sorry to jump on you, but it's <u>extremely</u> fragile. I took it out of the box over a year ago and I'm surprised it's still holding together."

"Oh. Sorry. My bad. It's a very unusual piece."

"Thanks.   I love finding art in the relatively common nature of everyday objects. Now, let me introduce you to the House of Pussy." Kitty leads you into a front sitting room and stops. She turns to face you. "Wait right here for a second while I find something *naughty* to show you."   A furtive smile flashes across her beautiful face and she turns and disappears down an adjacent hallway.

Oh hell yeah! you think. *Something "naughty"… hmmm.* Your mind goes wild with pictures of complex lacy black lingerie you've seen that boils your blood and sets your junk on fire. *God, I hope it's crotchless! No need even to remove it!*

With Kitty gone, you might as well use this time to start undressing.   No sense in holding up the party with your disrobing.   You remove your jacket and toss it on a nearby chair. You loosen your tie and pull the knot down giving you access to your shirt below. Slowly you unbutton your shirt, starting at the top, undoing each button in sequence. Maybe

You pull back and give Dixie's ass a little slap. She turns her head back and pouts at you, making you feel slightly ashamed of your manhood. She bounds back to the couch and gets up on all fours.

"Hit me, you pussy. Spank me. Spank me hard! Spank me like you mean it. Be a fucking man about it!" Dixie growls sexually at you through clenched teeth. "I have been a very bad girl, and you need to SPANK me!"

You pull back your open hand again and hit her a little harder on her perfect ass, releasing a sensual whimper in return. Come to think of it, you realize, it kinda does turns you on! You hit her again, this time even harder– the slap echoing off the walls of the living room. She groans again, louder, clearly enjoying it. You lift her dress at the leg slit and slide the opening over her ass, revealing two well-formed cheeks, smooth and round, something you typically only get with Photoshop. God, you just want to fuck that sweet ass. You haul back and smack her bare bottom with your palm, this time leaving a red hand print behind. She squeals and that does it. Your libido has reached the breaking point. You're going to mount this bitch here and now! You reach down to your pants, unzip your fly and–

A door crashes into the wall as it is flung open violently in the hallway just out of sight. Dixie jerks with a start, frantically reaching back to pull her dress back down to cover her reddened rear. You're largely stunned, not quite sure what to do. Dixie flips herself over to sit on the couch.

Before you can act, the burliest woman you've ever seen heaves into view from the hallway. She's wearing black, baggy cargo pants and a ribbed wifebeater that covers enormous tits which sag under their own weight. On her feet, black Army boots stomp the floor underneath with each step. Both arms are completely covered in mono-chromatic tattoos and the she-beast sports a buzz cut commonly found only on military personnel. *What the fuck have we awoken?!*

Dixie, looking innocent, asks, "Oh my. Did we wake you up, Margie honey?" *Wait, did she just say 'Margie'?* The tattoo is suddenly making a lot more sense.

Margie glowers at you with venomous eyes from across the room, seething in anger. Her fists clench, reopen and then clench into fists again– fists that you are a little worried might be used on you unless you do something like now!

You stammer quickly, "Hi Margie. Uh... we were... um... listen, I'm really sorry if we woke you up. See, I met Dixie at the martini bar down the street. We hit it off so we came back here to talk some. But I... uh...well, I guess that we were a tad loud, so I REALLY want to apologize for waking you up. That was very rude of us, of me especially, and well, I... uh...." you glance down at your bare chest and unbuttoned pants, your bikini underwear peeking through your unzipped fly. You look back up at Margie and zip up your fly, laughing nervously.

"It's Marge to you, asshole." Marge says slowly through clenched teeth, the muscles of her neck standing out. A vein pulses vividly on her forehead.

"Yes, 'Marge'. Of course, my apologies." You turn stiffly toward Dixie, "Well, I... uh... it was nice to meet you Dixie, but I... um... well, best be heading off then. See you all later." You smile wanly and wave pathetically to Dixie whose eyes are filled with fear and apology. You reach down to grab your stuff off the floor.

Before you can blink an eye, Marge comes barreling across the room, much faster than you ever expected the big woman could, and plants one of her Aryan Nation boots into your exposed chest between the two flaps of cloth that remain of your shirt. You go flying backwards, your shirt flapping like the sails of a boat cruising the ocean amidst gale force winds. You crash to the ground, gasping for air.

The stomping of Marge's boots vibrates the floor beneath your head as she plods over to where you lay. Above her footsteps you can make out Dixie's protests and desperate overtures to leave you alone. You open your eyes with trepidation as your breath starts to return through labored gasps. Marge is looming over you, a beefy tree of a woman.

"Nobody fucks my Dixie but ME!" she screams at you as one of her boots slams into your face, catching and breaking your nose before you get your arm up to deflect some of the kick.

You roll to the side as the second kick comes, digging into your lower back, striking your kidney. You arch your back in pain. Dixie meanwhile has interjected herself between you and Marge in a vain attempt to placate the sasquatch. The two of them argue heatedly which gives you a moment to get to your knees and waver to your feet.

Ignoring the rest of your clothing, you make a break for the door, getting so far as touching the knob before a meaty paw strikes you again in the same kidney causing you to reel backwards. Marge throws another punch, this time connecting with your face as you spin around. You drop to the floor. Marge drops her whole body weight onto your torso, her knee skillfully finding your nuts. She then proceeds to beat you for the next ten minutes or so until you thankfully pass out from the pain.

When you come to, you find yourself in the hallway, completely naked, your few vestiges of clothing gone. Blood soaks the right side of your head and mats your hair to your scalp. Every motion is greeted with tortuous pain. Every part of your body aches from the beating you received. You want to cry out but are fearful it will bring the beast for a second round. Instead, you groan as low and quietly as you can, exerting all the restraint you have left.

Through great effort, you make it to your feet, stumbling a few times into the hallway walls. You lurch down the hallway, finally knocking weakly on a door at the far end– far enough you hope, that Marge won't hear. After what seems like an eternity, a light comes on, shining a thin ray of hope under the door.

The door opens a crack, and a diminutive, wizened old face peers through the crack below the chain that holds the door secure.

"I think I need a doctor," is all you can muster. And having delivered your single appeal for help, you crumple to the floor and pass out.

The End

"Hey baby, watch out! There's a rooster in my pants, and my cock'll-do-you-too!" you say with suave enthusiasm.

She stares at you for a second then replies in a deadpan tone, "Ha. That's a... uh... good one. Yup." A weak courtesy laugh escapes her lips. She shakes her head with pity for you, then turns back to her drink, disregarding you entirely. *Shit. Wrong tactic.*

"Wait wait wait. I'm sorry," you apologize, backpedaling. "That was wicked retarded of me. You're obviously a woman with panache, and such a trite attempt on my part was just sad. How about I start over?" you suggest. You introduce yourself.

The woman obviously can't decide whether or not you're really worth talking to. After an uncomfortable pause, she eventually speaks up. "I'm Helen. Nice to meet you." She offers a hand which you shake politely. *Progress to be sure, but this is starting to feel like a business meeting. Shaking hands, really?!*

You glance at your watch. *Dammit!* Closing time is almost here and if you don't want to sleep alone, you need to change this situation and quick.

Helen turns back to her drink. You take a sip of yours to bide some time and figure out what to do next.

Tell a funny story.
Turn to page 291

Say something intelligent.
Turn to page 114

Chicks love dudes who know how to dress, so I'm thinking it's time for the suit, you decide. In the back of your closet, still in its plastic shroud from the dry cleaners, is your black, pin-striped suit. *A nice wrapping needs to showcase a great package,* you tell yourself as you grab your string bikini underwear. You select the one with the sculptured pouch in front to make your junk look HUGE for the lucky lady that will be experiencing it later tonight.

You reach in and grab out a long-sleeved, crisp white shirt and your suit. *Hmmm, which tie? Yeaaaaah, this one will do nicely.* You pull out a tie with tons of little squiggles decorating the front– it's a repeating pattern of the Ebola virus. There's no chance in hell that anyone will recognize it, but you feel it adds to your deadly look. *I'm gonna ravage me some bitches tonight,* you tell yourself smugly.

You take a visit to the bathroom for a little pomade to give you that wild animal look to your hair and decide to forgo shaving, intending your three day stubble to help counteract the put-together look of your suit. The finale is a little cologne, just a touch to give that subtle manliness to your whole look. *Pull 'em in with the eyes, seal the deal with the smell.*

Now the question is… how to approach the night. You could go alone– after all, you want to be the leading man tonight, not a supporting actor. However, having a wingman <u>might</u> be nice too. Hmmmm… you could ask your roommate Thad. He'd be fun to go out with. Or, come to think of it, there are tons of other friends you could call which might be fun to bring along, each having their own advantages to getting you laid.

Leg extended, you sweep the back of both his legs. His slick-soled boots lose purchase causing him to crack hard onto his back. The fall knocks the wind out him and you quickly take the opportunity to drop your elbow onto his solar plexus, keeping him from catching his breath.

You stand up, towering over the fallen giant.

"What up Motherfucker! You thought you could take this?!" you scream at him, adrenaline coursing through your veins.

Beltbuckle Bitch rolls over and starts to push himself up, his tight pants and slippery boots making it slow and difficult. Without sparing a thought, you kick him with all the force you can muster in the ribs. A sickening crack rings through the air and you can feel your foot moving into his chest cavity. The force of your kick flips him over dramatically, just like in the Kung fu movies. He crumples up on the floor in the fetal position, moaning.

"That's right, bitch! You better stay your monkey ass on the floor!" You're shaking from the adrenaline built up in the quick fight. Your hands are clenched so tight you can feel your nails digging into your palms. You straighten your tie again and smooth it down over your shirt, take a deep breath, and hold it for a second before letting it out.

You turn back to Loretta, her eyes wide, and take your coat back.

"Shall we?" you ask Loretta and proffer your arm.

Loretta takes your arm meekly and leans in whispering "My hero!" before pecking you on the cheek. Your hold your head high in a show of dominance to the crowd.

The two of you start back proudly toward your table. A rift develops just feet in front of you, closing quickly behind, as you pass through the enormous crowd that has developed. On the way, Loretta leans in close to talk privately.

"Listen, champ. We better go. Teddy has a ton of friends here and they're gonna kick your ass if you stay. I've got a car. What say we get outta here?"

"Fuck that, I could take 'em. Didn't you just see me back there, or did you blink when I knocked that guy the fuck out?" you boast loudly so that everyone can hear.

Ignoring your show, Loretta persists, "I think we should leave."

You reach your table to joyous accord and a stinging high-five from Thad. Loretta waves at Thad half-heartedly and then tugs your arm toward the door, motioning with her head to leave. Instead you pull your arm free and take a hard pull of beer from your glass. You lean in toward your roommate so that Loretta can't hear.

"Lissen bud, I guess we're outta here," you tell him. "You know chicks, some of 'em just can't wait to bed a cockjockey like myself." Thad just smiles, importing with his eyes that you are a lucky bastard.

"Alrighty then, stud. Just don't fuck her without a rubber."

"Yeah yeah," you reply. You turn toward Loretta. "Ok honey, where'd ya park? Let's go." You take one more swig

Dear Gentle Reader,

It is with great apology that I, your humble author, do take note with the events that unfold. You, with all your primal carnal urges, obviously have taken certain sexual liberties that need not retelling. Your repeated base acts utilizing positions that most only lust after, give cause for me to make only the slightest reference to them for your own remembrance. Dare I recall the many ways that one can enter a woman and your complete disregard for traditional methodology? In good conscience I cannot.

Suffice to say, there were many, MANY acts of sexual gratification that were employed in your encounter; and the couch, on and about which these acts were perpetrated, is of such a soiled condition that it will want of a deep cleaning. The events that transpired will become the stuff of drunken tales told during the wee hours of the morning after copious libations are consumed and tall tales emerge from inebriated bar patrons. Few will believe the events that you enacted upon the willing woman; but I, the omniscient recorder, have cause to simply state that while I applaud your manhood, I revile with hidden envy your activities of the evening.

With Regards,
Your Humble Author

The End

"Actually, what say you drop me off first. Would that be cool, Jules?"

"Sure bud. No problem."

Right on. This'll go great. You'll get out, tap on her window, and invite Ginnie up for a nightcap. How can she refuse? She's totally into you, you can tell.

Within minutes, Julie pulls up in front of your place. *Here we go.*

You step out of the car, trying to act less drunk that you really are. Before you close your door, (don't want Julie to drive away just yet!) you tap on Ginnie's window. She rolls it down with an inquisitive look on her face. You lean down to talk to her.

"What can I do for ya?" Ginnie asks.

"Hey, I wanted to see if you'd be interested in coming in. You know, we could get a little drink? Watch some bad, late night movie on TV? Whadda ya say?"

Ginnie smiles at you. "Listen, you're very nice and VERY drunk. As it turns out though, I think I already have my plans set for tonight." She looks over at Julie who smiles back. Ginnie then places her hand on Julie's knee and gently leans over to give her a kiss. She comes back to the window. "Sorry champ."

Julie smiles over at you from behind Ginnie and then drives away, the back door slamming shut on its own.

You stand there– stunned. *What the hell just happened? Julie is... gay?* You think back to all the years you've known her: middle school, high school, her softball games, all her "special friends" that you weren't allowed to meet. *Dammit. She is totally gonna hook up tonight! She was supposed to help ME get some. Argh.*

Head hung low, you walk back to your darkened house. *Oh well, I guess one in the hand is better than two bumpin' bush.*

The End

"Nah nah. I'm all good. You can take Ginnie home first."

Julie looks at Ginnie and she shrugs.

"Fine by me," Ginnie says. "The more the merrier!" Both girls giggle and you laugh along despite the fact you feel you're left out of some inside joke.

After twenty minutes, you get to Ginnie's condo. Surprisingly, Julie parks the car rather than just letting Ginnie get out. Not quite what you were expecting.

"You coming in?" Ginnie asks.

"Uh... yeah. Of course. That'd be great," you stammer, confused.

You, Julie and Ginnie go up to her third floor condo. It's retardedly nice. Ginnie has great taste in decorating and you find yourself a little ashamed of your bachelor pad. Probably a good thing you didn't show Ginnie your place first.

Ginnie and Julie sit down on a black velvet couch at the edge of a sprawling bear's head rug. Ginnie picks up a remote, punches a button and a fire springs to life in the hearth just beyond the rug. *Wow, how romantic,* you think. *God, if I can just get rid of Julie, we can get this night started!*

"Hey, where's the pisser... I mean, toilet?" you ask.

"Around there. Third door on the right," Ginnie answers congenially.

You leave the two of them to talk as you hit the head, all the while hatching various plans to get Julie the hell outta there. After taking a leak, you straighten yourself in the mirror, polishing your look, fixing your hair. *Ok... SHOWTIME!* You exit the bathroom and return to the living room.

HOLY SHIT! You can't believe your eyes. It's... beyond belief. *What the fuck is going on?* You're transfixed, standing there in the hallway. Before you, on the couch are Julie and Ginnie and they're no longer talking– they're KISSING!

"Uh... excuse me. Sorry, I... uh... um... you're a lesbian, Julie?!" you ask, dumbfounded.

Julie stops, one arm enveloping Ginnie whose hand is resting gently on Julie's enormous rack. "Yup. Sorry to surprise you," she says with a glint in her eye. All of a sudden it all falls into place– high school, the softball team, Julie's "special friends", and now her actions tonight with Ginnie.

"Wanna join?" asks Ginnie.

Again, thunderstruck. This is it. The holy grail of fantasies. Two chicks... at the SAME time! Your mouth is moving but no words are coming out. *Is this a dream? Am I that drunk that I'm making all this up?*

"I... I... well, uh... yeah. I think that would be cool," you respond slowly, hesitant to break the spell.

What transpired next is one of the coolest tales you have to share with your buds over poker for the next ten years. The three of you had crazy passionate (and in your case, drunken) sex like you've never dreamed possible. There were positions and partners and well, holy shit. It was freakin' amazing!

The End

Quick as you can, you turn to make a play for the gun. The lateness of the hour and the sway of the cab have lured Margaret into a bit of a highway hypnosis, so she doesn't respond quick enough. You plant your hand on top of the gun and force it down so that if it fires, it won't hit you.

Click! Margaret pulls the trigger. The hammer slams down on the skin between your thumb and forefinger, blocking the gun from firing. You grit your teeth with the pain but refuse to relinquish your hold. The two of you struggle. The driver yells back to Margaret, but you're too involved to make out what he's saying.

Suddenly, both of you are thrown forcefully against the Plexiglas divider separating the front seat from the back. Evidently James has slammed on the brakes to help Margaret deal with her situation. The side of your face hurts from colliding with the Plexiglas, but you know that you need to do something quick or you'll soon be outnumbered and probably killed.

You look at the woman next to you. It seems that her impact with the divider has broken her nose. Blood gushes out like a garden hose, covering her mouth and dripping thickly off her chin. Groggy, she's fumbling around on the floor with her hand, trying to locate the dropped gun.

The front door opens and James steps out, swearing. You reach over and lock your door moments before he opens it. You shuffle your feet around on the floor to impede Margaret's search and in doing so, you feel them connect with something hard, hopefully the gun. You throw out your elbow, connecting violently with Margaret's temple, sending her reeling backwards. You then turn, grab her by the back of her head and slam her face again into the Plexiglas. Again and again, you smash her beautiful face unrelentingly against the thick wall until you hear the exterior window next to you break. It's the driver!

You release Margaret and bend down to scoop up the small pistol. You push back against the unconscious woman, raise the gun and fire toward the window, hitting the driver in the face as he attempts to enter the car.

Blood explodes as the bullet rips through his nose into his brain. He falls partway into the backseat through the broken window, impaling himself on the shards of splintered glass. His head hangs down and blood pours out from the hole in his face, pooling on the seat beside you.

You turn and crawl over Margaret to get out of the taxi. Your hands shake uncontrollably from the massive amounts of adrenaline coursing through your body. You put the gun in your pocket and drag Margaret from the back seat onto the side of the road. You then walk around the back of the cab and pull the driver from the shattered window. He falls unceremoniously on the pavement like a sack of potatoes and lays there, one arm outstretched above his head.

You pull the gun from your pocket and open it to see if there are any bullets left. There aren't, so you wipe it down with your shirt to remove any fingerprints like you've seen a thousand times on TV. You then throw it over in Margaret's direction and get into the taxi.

The keys are still in the ignition, thank God, so you start the car and get the fuck out of there, not completely sure what you're going to do next.

The End

"Actually, I think I'm ready to cash in now, if you wouldn't mind waiting a second."

"Definitely sir. If you prefer, you can leave your chips on the table. We will cash them in for you and deposit them at a bank of your choice or execute a cashier's check for your winnings."

"Sure. Thanks. Um… whatever's fine." You start to follow the casino employee when you feel a tap on your shoulder. You turn back to see the woman who was standing next to you at the craps table.

"Mind if I tag along? I think I made you an offer that you have yet to redeem," the woman in the golden dress says smiling.

"Indeed I don't. Shall we?" You proffer your elbow which she hooks her arm into and the two of you follow the sharp dressed man.

Waiting for you is the most grandiose suite you have ever laid eyes upon. Tall ceilings float above opulent furnishings that must rival that of the British Royal Family. You can't help but smiling, your cheeks hurt from how wide your grin is. You flop face down on the heavenly bed, the soft mattress feels like a cloud underneath, removing the fatigue which is finally catching up to you.

"Are you sleepy, my big winner?"

You roll over to see a golden dress on the floor and a svelte nude body standing beside it. Long luscious hair, released from its capture, cascades over perfect shoulders, framing the face of classic beauty.

"Or would you like one more perk?"

The End

You look around to find the cab stand and it's hell and far gone from where you got dropped off. There are hardly any people around. It's the airport's dead hours– past the time of most departures and before the arrival of red-eyes. You whistle softly in an attempt to perk up a little after fucking up the night so badly. The loneliness of your current environment is a real buzz kill for your drunken self.

You wait and wait at the cab stand; until finally, you get tired of standing and sit down on the curb. Hmmm... maybe you should call a taxi service to see if they're still running and let them know that you're waiting out here. You check your watch and almost an hour has gone by since Sofia left. You put your elbows on your knees, fold your arms on top of one another and put your head down. The relaxing effects of the booze make you sleepy.

After who knows how long, you hear the sound of an ill-kept engine rumbling toward you. You lift your head to see a taxi finally appear. *It's about fucking time!* The cab pulls up and you open the door to get in.

"Hey! Hold up there!"

You turn to see a woman exiting the airport, jogging toward you. She is clad in a black trench coat tied at the waist, a hint of her dress showing through at the top. She wears precariously tall heels, ones definitely not made for cab catching. You're somewhat wondering/hoping to see if she's gonna take a spill on the way to reach you.

"Hey! Excuse me! Can I share that taxi with you?" the dark-haired woman asks, almost to the cab. Slightly winded from her jog, she presses, "Are you going toward the city? It's hell trying to catch a cab out here at this time of night, so I'd love to share your cab with you if you're heading that way." Your place isn't really in the city, but it's close enough that dropping her off won't be that far out of the way. On the other hand, it's been a helluva night and getting home sooner rather than later would be nice.

Let her share the taxi.
Turn to page 340

Tell that bitch to get her own damn cab!
Turn to page 127

Ok, you decide, *Loren/Loretta's gender is not going to be a big deal. Best to put that issue aside as there is a much bigger, <u>life-threatening</u> issue at hand.*

"So Loren, here's what needs to happen. You're a dude and I'm guessing you have balls, so it's time to use 'em. First, your mascara is running horribly, and I don't think I can deal with you looking like some pathetic beauty queen that came in second at prom. You gotta take care of that shit. Second, we need to figure out just what the fuck we're gonna do. There are four guys out there that want to beat me to death, and I'm guessing that they're not real progressive, accepting folk; so we *both* need a way out."

"I agree. Maybe we sho– DUCK!" Loren shrieks as headlights suddenly enter the garage.

The two of you slouch farther down into your seats as a pickup truck drives slowly by, modern country music blaring from the opened windows. It looks like you've caught a break as the truck continues up the towering parking garage.

"I've got a plan," Loren says suddenly, breaking the tense silence of the moment. "But you're going to need to trust me. I know where we can go that is safe, but you can't go dressed like that."

"What? What do you mean, 'dressed like this'? I look great for just about ANY situation, including my own funeral it seems."

"You're going to need to trust me," Loren reiterates. "Get out and meet me at the trunk."

Loren opens his door and slinks out. You stall for a second, your mind reeling as to what Loren has in mind. You draw a complete blank. Getting out of the car, you wince at the thunderous groan the car door makes, especially with the good 'ol boys so close.

You make your way to the trunk which is now open and has Loren bent over in it, rummaging around noisily.

"Here we go! I knew it was still back here," Loren comments to himself out loud.

With a satisfied smile, Loren pulls out a freshly dry cleaned, beautiful, yellow, silken gown with large, red hibiscus flowers on it. The dress is still on the hanger and covered in a thin plastic shroud. He pushes the dress at you. Next, he pulls out a jet black, straight-haired Asian wig and red high heel pumps.

"I told you you'd have to trust me. Put it on," Loren demands. "And be quick about it, they'll be back any minute now!"

No way in HELL!
Turn to page 125

Put the goddamn dress on.
Turn to page 297

This bitch is fucking crazy! You brush by Foxy, bounding for the front door.

"Stop!" she screams. "Stop!"

You hear an audible metallic click and an explosion that rings your ears. A huge chunk of wall explodes next to you leaving a hole the size of an orange in the drywall. *Oh FUCK!* Realizing you just got really fucking lucky, you leap for the front door which is only a few feet away, hoping to get out before she can pull off another round.

"That is NOT the way to Sanctuary! I've tried that door, and it does not go to Sanctuary!!"

You completely ignore her screams and fling open the front door. **BOOM!** Another shot goes off and a searing pain racks your body, stemming from the new hole ripped through your leg. You fall out the door onto the porch and wince in horrible pain. She shot you through your thigh, your black pants darken with the outpouring of blood. *Oh* sparit wid an ease of voice dat laves one's ears pining fa mahr."

Dixie blushes slightly, and her smile grows ever wider. "Well, I could say the same about your accent! It's so sexy hearing you speak English but like, NOT speak English." She giggles at her own joke and you join in with a courtesy laugh.

"Tha ohnleh diffahrance is that I be speekin' the Queen's anglish while yew speak the tongue of the colonies."

"Oh silly. We're not colonies anymore! We're a country!" You smile at her comment, a little taken aback by her grade school interpretation. You take a long sip of your martini. *Better keep the conversation rather shallow. She's clearly no Einstein.*

You set your martini down and take a small step backward to better view this luscious beauty next to you. "Well nah, lemme be tahkin' a good look at cher gown. At's an Armani... no wait, et's a Diane von Furstenberg af I'm noht mistahken. Smashing. Trulah smashing. N' I see that ye gots yerself a one of them tattoos. Who moight be 'Margie'?"

Dixie instinctively looks down at the name 'Margie' tattooed in spotty blue/black ink just above her ankle. It's poorly inked as if done by an amateur. She hastily moves to cross her legs such that the tattoo is removed from view.

"It's nothing. I'm a little embarrassed that you even saw it. It's from another time in my life, a time I'm not very proud of."

"Na, dohna be all embahrassed on my account. Et's not all dat bad. Is Margie ah friend ah yers?"

"Yes, but I really don't want to talk about it. "

"Fair 'nuf, fair 'nuf. Ain't nuthin' but a whistle to a tea kettle. So, can a chap buy ya anuther of watever ya be trinkin'?"

Quickly, Dixie downs the almost full glass of Limoncello and remarks, "Why yes. That would be lovely." A small burp escapes her lips, and she raises her hand late to cover it demurely. "I seem to find myself without a drink!" *Holy*

Mary, Mother of God! She downed that drink like a frat boy suckin' on a beer bong during Rush Week simply in response to my invitation for another. Well, at least getting her tanked shouldn't be too much of an issue!

"My plahsure than," you say and order up another for Dixie. Over the next hour or two, you continue your conversation– lightly delving into your imaginary past in England, her sense of style, movies and a few other vacuous conversation topics that are largely forgettable. You're still kinda curious about her taboo tattoo, but her meaningful attempts to keep it hidden stops you from pursuing its story further at this point.

After more than a few Limoncellos for her and martinis for yourself, you know the iron is hot. It's time to make your move. However, before you can structure your exit strategy with Dixie, she speaks up.

"What say you and I fuckin' go back to my place and fuckin' take this party to the next LEVEL!" *Oh yeah, she's definitely liquored up.* "That ok with you, ya limely bastard?" Dixie lets out a boisterous laugh and sways slightly, awaiting your response.

Ask her again about her tattoo.
Turn to page 321

Go with her.
Turn to page 327

Time to cut bait– this one is a little too wild for the hook. "Will now, ya be a wee bit fohrward now arn't ya? Ee dohn't be enjoyin' ya callin' me a poof, not neither! What see ya be runnin' aloong na lass." You make a little "scoot away" motion with your fingers. "I canna no see meself goin' home with sooch a foul cunt."

"Excuse me?! You <u>didn't</u> just call me a 'cunt', did you?" Dixie's temper flares. Her hitherto pale skin now glows red with rage at your comment.

You pause in assessment. This is obviously a moment to heed the immortal words of Thad the Roommate: Rather than beating around the bush for a while, it's best to just set the bush ablaze. "How about I say it in an American accent then: you prison handle-fucking broom whore, I don't want to go home with you," you say dramatically, dropping the tiresome English-ish accent.

Dixie is stunned, bowled over at your perfect American accent AND being told off so bluntly. She reaches for her glass to throw her drink on you, but thankfully it's empty. A few drops of Limoncello spatter against your face. Dixie slings the glass to the floor where it crashes with an expensive tinkle, turns, and storms away. You smile– mission accomplished.

You wipe away the drops of sticky success from your face and signal to the nearest waitress for another martini. You look down at your watch. *Uh oh,* you realize, *it's getting late and this dick sure isn't going to suck itself. Last call is just around the corner. Time to cast the net a little wider.*

You throw your eyes around the room, surveying what boat trash is left on deck. *Hmmmmm... there, at the far end of the bar, she'll do.* You smile. You've never gone after an older woman but hey, supposedly they make up in experience what they have lost in looks. Desperate and divorced– a sure recipe for nookie in the male playbook.

Sitting at the bar, a bit to one end, is an elegant woman probably in her late forties or perhaps early fifties, very well kept, a real eyefuck of an older woman. Examining her looks and behavior, she strikes you as a bit of a cougar. She is dressed in a conservative white blouse and dark pencil skirt. Green, snake-skin stiletto heels wrap around her feet which she kicks casually, one well-cut leg over the other, sitting at the bar. Occasionally, she plays with the gold chain around her neck while looking around. Thankfully, your eyes don't meet. That would be creepy and weird. She sighs, a sure sign for you to move in.

Now, reflecting over what you've heard, older chicks tend to fall into one of two camps. On the one side, you have women who love to pretend they're still young– reliving their days of flirting when they could turn heads, giggling at ridiculous pickup lines used by drunk twenty-something suitors. On the other hand, she may be one of those stuck up bitches who's just looking for a good fuck from a man that needs no assistive pills.

You grab your newly arrived drink and saunter toward her, flashing the smile that's bedded a thousand women. She notices you and smiles a confident grin in return. You approach her and say…

_____

A no-nonsense statement that gets to the point.
Turn to page 287

A cheesy pickup line.
Turn to page 202

Oral hygiene is my specialty! Let's go!
Turn to page 233

Whaddabout somewhere else?
Turn to page 78

You arrive at an upscale dental practice, a detached building with a sleek front of brushed metal and frosted glass. You whistle softly. *Somebody's got some money!* Helen rummages through her small purse and pulls out a keycard which she swipes over a black plastic pad just outside the door. A little LED light on the black pad turns from red to green, and you hear the thick glass door unlatch. Helen pulls it open with the brushed nickel pull. It swings patiently, rotating on a huge metal pole that runs through the last quarter of the door.

The two of you go inside– a lofted, airy lobby decorated in a Mid-Century Modern style greets you. A broad, wooden coffee table with thin metallic legs sits awash with current magazines in the middle of the room. Comfy couches straddle the walls. An enormous saltwater fish tank sits flush above one couch, a glimpse into a perfect sea. Within, bright fish swim among gnarled coral; bubbles creep up from the white pebbled bottom. The tank's glow lights the room.

"Now close your mouth and stop gawking. Yes, yes, it's all very nice, but what we want is this way." Helen goes past a generous, black granite reception counter and pulls open the only other door in the space. A darkened hallway greets you. You follow Helen into the darkness, the last vestiges of light departing as the door swings silently shut behind you.

Helen grabs your hand and leads you blindly down the corridor. Partway down, she stops. You hear a jingle of keys and a door opening. Helen grabs your hand again and leads you into a room.

The lights sputter on and you find yourself in a dentist's office, its multi-functional chair sits right in the middle. The office is not altogether large, and the white walls are decorated with framed prints of Picasso's work. A large lamp on an articulating arm extends from the wall, and a tray of instruments neatly laid out on a metal table is off to one side. A huge picture window graces the far wall, showing the forestry that backs up to the rear of the office. It's a serene scene of huge oaks, their leaves tempered with moonlight that trickles down among them.

Helen jumps into the chair and lies down on her back. Her breasts rise like volcanic cones that sit above a sea of designer clothing.

"Come to me," Helen commands and you mount her. She reaches up to you, pulling your face down to hers. The two of you kiss fervently. Each of you undresses the other until both of you are naked, clearly aroused by the other's company.

Helen then gently directs you into a number of different positions, things you never considered with women in the past. Some are fun, others are challenging, but all are enlightening in their approach to a time-honored activity. At one point, she has you on your hands and knees, leaning back against her upraised legs, your cock pushing down and back into her moist reception. Another time, she straddles you lying down toward your feet, her legs bent and her feet on your chest. You enter her from behind as she pushes back against your member, placing you deep within her. It's ecstatic and you close your eyes, taking in the incredible feeling each time you enter her. At long last, you groan in sync with Helen, both of you orgasming together. *Holy shit that was incredible!*

For minutes afterwards, the two of you just allow the orgasm wash over you, neither one of you moving, letting your bodies enjoy the rush.

"Helen, is that you?" a deep voice bellows from down the hall. *What the fuck!*

"Oh shit, it's my husband!" Helen whispers hoarsely to you. "He can't find you here. He's really jealous and will kill you if he finds out you fucked me."

"What?! Me fuck you? Wait, this was your idea! This was all your idea! OH SHIT!" You frantically pull out of Helen, causing her to gasp, and leap over to shut the door.

"Does this door lock?" you ask Helen. A pounding sounds on the other side followed by a jiggle of the door handle.

"Yes, it's locked, but Donald has a key so it's only seconds until he comes in!" *Oh fuck. Oh fuck. Oh fuck.*

"Helen, let me in! I can't see a goddamn thing out here! So help me God, if you're fucking another boy-toy on my chair, I swear to Christ in Heaven above that I'm going to gut the two of you and bury you in the woods out back!" You shoot Helen a shocked glance. *This is a habit of hers?*

You look around the room madly, seeking anything that might help you out. Your eyes settle on the tray of tools off to the side– little drills, metal spikes, stainless steel pliers– a bountiful wealth of items to torture you with. *Oh holy fuck, what have I gotten myself into?* you think.

Keys jingle out in the hallway, and you hear one sliding into the lock. The handle shakes but doesn't turn– the wrong key. Donald swears, and you hear it being withdrawn.

"I'm going to tear you in half, you fucking slut! And the shit I'm going to do to whatever man you have in there is a page removed from the repertoire of Satan, himself. I'm going to bring Hell in there with me when I find the right goddamn key. I'm going to pull out each of your teeth one by one until you choke on the blood that will course down your whorish throat. How dare you threaten to divorce me and ruin me and then secretly fuck half of this city behind my back in my own goddamn office?!"

"You're such a pig-fucker, Donald!" Helen yells back at the door, fists clenched, still stark naked.

"You're NOT helping!" you scream at Helen in a low voice.

"Fuck him and his practice. He just likes to play golf and travel and buy stupid electronics. He's a BASTARD!" Helen says to you, screaming out the last word so that her husband can hear.

Another key slips into the lock. Your heart leaps up into your throat. The lock jiggles, but again the door doesn't open. Your pulse races. Your luck isn't going to last forever.

You look back at the tray and notice a container of putty and a UV light gun. *Filling material. That's it!* You grab the two items along with a metal tool that has a small pad at one end. You race to the door, just as another key is being removed with a slur of obscenities. With the metal tool you scoop out some putty and cram it into the keyhole. You scoop and cram as much as you can fit into the lock and then hold up the UV light to the keyhole, solidifying the filling material inside. The lock is now sealed shut, just like a newly filled molar.

You turn back to Helen who is casually dressing herself.

"What the fuck are you doing? Hurry up! That filling won't last forever. He's bound to knock the fucking door down at some point. You've really pissed him off royally!"

"Oh, he's such a blowhard. He won't hurt me. I've secreted away some dirt on him to a safety deposit box. If he ever does anything to me, my lawyer has a key. You... well... he might actually kill you, come to think of it," Helen says matter-of-factly.

You shake your head and sigh. *What the hell is going on with these rich fucks?* More pounding at door signals it's time to leave.

You grab your clothes and rapidly dress, just enough so you don't have to carry anything. You go over to the window and find that it does indeed open. With little effort, you unlatch the lock. The expensive window glides open with the merest push.

You look back at Helen who is almost completely dressed now and attempting to pacify Donald through the door. It really doesn't seem to have any effect save for keeping Donald engaged, a prime opportunity for you to get the hell out of there. Helen looks over at you and shoos you away with a flick of her hand. You duck out the window and run into the safety of awaiting forest.

Wow, that was...something, you think. You pause to catch your breath, safely surrounded by tall trees and silence, and vow to never go after older women again. *Those bitches are CRAZY!*

The End

you to do stupid things, and sometimes you really need that kick in the ass.

———————————

Call up Conservative Pete?
Turn to page 91

Call Party Dog Kevin?
Turn to page 238

Better to drown your misery at the bar with people than at home alone. You imagine you've got that feeling that sport fisherman get when the big one snaps the line at the last second just beyond the boat and disappears back under the sea. Maybe you should have gone to 'Brasil'. You sigh. *Oh well.*

You walk sullenly through the automatic sliding doors and make your way down toward Terminal C. Adjacent to security there lies a great little bar frequented by pilots, stewardesses and business travelers needing to tie one on before heading out. You slip in and sit at the bar.

The bartender saunters over and you order your first drink of many. Over the next few hours, you talk with the bartender about women, enumerating the many issues you have with them.

"Take the toilet seat for example. God forbid it's left up! Guys are always expected to put the seat back down after we go. I mean, hell, we put it up so we don't piss all over it. They should be thankful we put it up in the first place. So why can't a chick just be happy and put the damn thing back down? C'mon, all a bitch needs to do it give it a tap and gravity does the rest. Is it really such a fuckin' crime to leave the seat up?" Throughout your continuous rant, the bartender simply nods from time to time, smiling and agreeing.

Beer after beer comes your way, your glass never reaching empty before the next one appears. *Jesus Christ, this guy's a great, fuckin' bartender!* Smashed, you decide that you love this guy, not like in a gay way or anything, but like in a brotherly way. Dude's totally your bro. You decide you're going to tip him well when the end of the night comes.

Inevitably two a.m. rolls around and despite your sentimental feelings about the bartender, you are informed that it's closing time and you gotta go. You whine pathetically how you guys are bros now so you should get one more brew, but Johnny the Greatest Bartender EVER won't budge. After a few minutes you drunkenly acquiesce and stumble out into the airport proper, completely forgetting to tip your new friend.

Holy shit, you're drunk. You missed the greatest opportunity of your life and now you're fuckin' wasted in the airport. *This sucks*, you decide. You should do something. Fuck, you should go somewhere. *Yeah, I mean, I'm in an airport after all.* Then it comes to you– *Vegas. Fuck yeah, VEGAS BABY! Everybody gets lucky in Vegas.* You need to go to Vegas!

After some initial confusion where the ticket counters were, you make your way to the lone remaining agent who clearly hates his job.

"What the fuck do you want?" he asks.

"Hey hey hey. I'm a patron, bro. I want to fly the friendly skies. Here, here's my credit card. I want to go to fuckin' Vegas on the next possible flight." The ticket counter agent rolls his eyes and mutters something under his breath.

"There's one leaving here in forty minutes. Think you can manage to drag your drunk ass down to Concourse B, Gate 12 without too much trouble?"

"Hey, back up off the surliness there bud. What, do you hate your job? I know I hate mine. I sling coffee for a living. How cool is that?" you mention sympathetically, your drunken friendly nature not put off by the gate agent's attitude.

"Listen my drunk little friend. I work the graveyard shift at this lone, shithole counter. Most nights I'm relegated to dealing with people running from the law, running from a spouse and people who just need to 'get away' for a while. Looking at you, I can see that you most likely fall in the latter category. Now fuck off down to Gate 12 so I can go back to napping behind this counter. Have a pleasant day." He gives you back your credit card along with a ticket, boarding pass, and a mocking wave before disappearing behind the counter.

You head to the gate, easily passing through security since you have no baggage. The plane is already boarding when you get there. *Thank God the plane is almost empty.*

You find a row that is completely unoccupied and sit in the center. You buckle your seatbelt, put up the armrests on all sides, and promptly stretch out across all three seats. You fall asleep before the plane even takes off.

When you awaken, still remarkably drunk, you are in Sin City. The night has yet to end with the sun just under an hour from rising on a new day full of promise. From McCarran Airport you catch a taxi to the Bellagio. Soon you are cruising down the Strip, neon lights dance on the car windows from garish casinos on either side, beckoning you to come within. The light atop the Luxor pierces the early morning sky, seeking the sun, before the skyline of New York New York draws into view. You roll down the window, lean into the rushing wind and take in a deep breath of desert air. You hold it for second savoring it. You can taste the wealth all around. *Goddammit, it's time to turn my life around!*

Within minutes, the graceful, illuminated fountains of the Bellagio spray skyward in dance, signaling your arrival. Your taxi pulls up under the Old World European train station covering.

Departing the cab, you enter the Bellagio. The enormous lobby is decorated by fragile, colorful glass flowers overhead, giving you the feeling of being an ant beneath a field of poppies. There's no time to waste though. You head straight for the casino floor. The sound of slot machines singing out all around is a cacophonous orchestral score of chance. You open your wallet to check your funds– one hundred and sixty-eight dollars. You pull out your stash, push it into your pocket and straighten your tie. Let's gamble!

You wander through the casino, deciding what will deliver the fortune you so desperately crave. Almost as an omen, an older lady clad in an ill-fitting, bold, pink floral print dress sitting at the end of a bank of slot machines, gambling with her retirement savings and a possible future as a Walmart greeter, shrieks in joy as you pass by. You stop to watch as her slot machine spills its silvery guts. Dollar coins gush loudly into the tray below. The woman is ecstatic,

"Yeah, it's pretty sweet. I mean, I can't say much because it's all very hush hush with these government projects. But yeah, it's a great gig and fingers crossed... moon, here I come!"

She giggles musically. "That thar is boond to be an adventure ta be sure. Seein' as ya canna no talk aboot it, what say we hit the dance fleur. Ya do dance, don't ye?"

"Oh, most definitely. Hey, I didn't catch your name."

The redhead blushes slightly. "Where be ma manners? Ma name is Maggie altho me friends call me Mags."

"I like that, Mags. It's a fun name. What say we get to that dance now?"

The two of you make your way to the dance floor, heavily populated by people all moving in rhythm to the bouncing club music. You and Maggie dance, separate at first but within a few songs, Maggie is grinding up on you sexually, getting your libido raging. A few more songs and the two of you are virtually dryhumping on the dance floor. You know you want her bad, and it's more than obvious that she feels the same.

You spin her around and kiss her fully. Your lips press aggressively together, the pumping music driving your desire to take her here and now. She grabs your ass and pulls herself in, rubbing her waist against you, tempting you to go further.

Instantly you know you can't wait anymore and break away from your impassioned kiss. Maggie leans in close to your ear and whispers loudly above the deafening music, "God, I want you to fark me. Eem so wet, ya need to fark me NOW! We nad to leave."

You couldn't agree more. You take Maggie by the hand and make for the exit. Passing by the bar on your way out, you hope to see Kevin to let him know he needs to get his own ride home. You notice him at a high table, the top filled with drinks and his arms around twin blondes. He makes eye contact with you as you walk by, nods affirmatively and smiles. *He'll be just fine,* you think to yourself.

Once outside, you stop Maggie briefly. "Where do you want to go? We could head to my place? I've got a waterbed." You say enticingly.

Maggie returns your smile with raised eyebrows. "Ey donno. They be givin' me a wee bit of the seasickness, ya know. How eboot we 'ed ta ma place?"

———————————

If you insist on your place,
turn to page 60

If you decide to head to her place,
turn to page 255

You throw up your hands in an effort to give her pause. You speak quickly, "No, you don't understand! See, this woman Sam who works here said she wanted to show me some old maps here in the archives. She took me down here and then we fucked– I mean, sorry, had sex, and then she left me and took all my clothes and OH GOD, please don't call security. I didn't mean to startle you and if you would just– Holy Shit!" It suddenly dawns that you're buck naked while rapidly trying to explain your presence. Frantically, you snatch a book off the shelf and open it to cover yourself as best you can.

A little more calm now, the old librarian relaxes and her arm holding the radio drops to her side. She looks at you curiously, the initial shock fading.

You stutter on, "Honestly, ma'am. I, well, I'm sorry to be here all naked, but I'm totally lost and I've been down here for hours. I really just want to get out and get home and try to forget this whole night. Please ma'am. Please. Please don't have me arrested." Suddenly, you remember your proof.

"Oh, and wait a sec. Here, let me show you the note Sam left to show you I'm not lying. I mean, it doesn't say much, but you've got to believe me," you plead.

You hand the note to the librarian as best you can while trying to keep yourself covered. She takes it and gives it a cursory read.

"Son, there's no one who works down here named Sam."

"Oh I'm sorry. My bad. Her name is Samantha. Sam's just a nickname or something."

"Nope, nobody named Samantha either. Could be she was one of the cleaning people, I guess. They're here at night to give everything a good dusting."

Oh that bitch! you think furiously to yourself. *She wasn't even a librarian but a fuckin' cleaning person. Oh my God! I can't believe I was taken like that. Never again am I drinking.*

You snap back to the present to find the old librarian looking at you in an odd way. Confused, you can't quite figure out what she's doing. And then it hits you: *Oh God, she's sizing me up!*

To confirm your fears, the librarian says, "Listen, son. You're a fine lookin' man and it's been a long time I've been with a fine lookin' man. What say you treat me to a little nookie and I radio to security that everything is ok?" An evil grin breaks out on her face, disturbing her wrinkles to an even greater degree.

A wave a repulsion cascades through your body and you involuntarily shudder. *God. Jail or sex with Grandma Bookworm– those are my fucking choices? Jesus Christ, how can this get any worse?*

Fulfill Grannie's carnal desires.
Turn (Ugh) to page 65

Run like hell!
Turn to page 305

"How about this, honey? Why don't <u>you</u> choose and we'll both agree to abide by your decision," you propose.

"Fine by me," Beltbuckle chimes in with a challenging tone.

Loretta looks back and forth between the two of you, slowly going from one man to the other, sizing the both of you up. You straighten your tie and flash your most winning smile. You know she's going to pick you. *Poor schmuck*, you think about the other guy. *He never had a chance.*

Sure enough, after a few seconds, Loretta leans in close to you. You feel her hot breath tickling the little hairs on your ear. Through a barely audible whisper you hear her comment, "Pussy."

She then backs away, grabs the arm of Texas Fuckface and strolls away, stealing one last sneer toward you as she departs.

Your face starts to burn with embarrassment as everyone around you shakes their head at your fate. Tail between your legs, you walk back to your table and your awaiting roommate who's desperately trying to stifle a laugh at your expense.

"Dude, you should have clocked that chump! You could have taken him!"

"Yeah dude, totally. I should have decked that ass-fuck," you respond in a less than convincing tone. You feel horrible.

In an attempt to lift your spirits, Thad chimes in, "Hey, what say we hit that other club after all, you know, that 70's one?"

Take Thad's advice and hit Blaxploitation.
Turn to page 164

Fuck this, fuck her, fuck it all. Head home.
Turn to page 332

You get in your car and follow Maggie to her place. She's a great leader, being sure to stop at yellow lights so that you don't need to run the red. After a while, you notice that the city around you is becoming more and more run down– the dilapidated buildings and seedy inhabitants growing in number by the block. You become a little concerned about Maggie's welfare living in such a shithole area. Well, if things go really well, maybe she'll consider meeting at your house next time.

Maggie parks her car on the street outside a rundown tenement building. There's garbage strewn along the curb which festers in a swill of dirty water. You park behind her, a bit worried that your car might be boosted in this section of town. It's not like your car is really all that nice; but shit, it's just about the nicest car you've seen in the past ten minutes driving here. Not a good sign.

"Hey Mags, no offense but is it safe for you to live here? I mean, you're a very pretty girl and I'd be kinda sketched if I were you," you tell her.

"Eh, no worries aboot that. E've got me mace with me and I took a self-difence carse. Yer not a wee bit scarred now, are ya?"

"No no. I can handle my own, no problem," you say with more confidence than you have. You change the subject.

"So, will my car be safe here?"

"Ain't a problem, boyyo" Maggie replies with a smile. "Now what say we be hadin' inside to fark sum!" Maggie pulls out her keys from the clutch she's carrying. A small bottle of mace and whistle come out attached to the keychain. You're a little relieved to know that she wasn't exaggerating about the mace.

Maggie jiggles the key in the building door's lock, cursing under her breath. After a little struggle, the mud smudged glass door unbolts and the two of you enter the foyer. She opens her narrow brass mailbox with an ear-piercing squeak from rusted hinges and checks for mail. The

With a slight apprehension you get out of the car, a tad worried what "surprise" Helen has in store for you. However, your curiosity is piqued, so you just go with it.

"Not much travel business these days?" you ask Helen, gesturing to the outdated, fluorescent-colored window lettering that has certainly seen better days.

"Oh, plenty of travel! The big thing now is that I no longer have to advertise," Helen says proudly. She turns a brass key with a loud click to open the glass door of the travel agency.

"So, just for the record, I really have no interest in starring in a snuff film. I just want to put that out there," you toss off jokingly with a nervous edge to your voice.

Helen chuckles. "Don't worry. No basements with ball gags and gimps here. Now c'mon in and I'll fix us a drink."

Despite your better judgment, you really could use a drink to steady your nerves. You follow Helen into the travel agency. She flicks on the overhead fluorescents which cast the office in a sterile, greenish hue. You take a look around.

The office has an open feel to it– two desks with consultation chairs on the opposite side greet visitors to the agency. Both desks have a phone and an outdated beige computer sitting on them. There are a series of travel brochures in little plastic containers that line the right wall. Many of them are for places around the US with a smaller number designated for European or Asian destinations. You idly walk over to the Asian section and pick up one of the brochures. Inside, using somewhat poor grammar, the wonders of the area are touted: the fine shopping, the historic sights, the exotic food. It's mildly interesting information although you notice the fashions in the photos are quite outdated, probably from the 1980's judging from the Jam Pants and crimped hair.

You are startled by the heavy glass door being slammed closed and the loud metallic thunk of the door's lock being engaged. When you look over, Helen asks nonchalantly, "Ever been to Asia?" *Why is she locking us in?* you wonder.

"No, never. I'd love to go someday though." You set the flyer back into its slot and wander to the middle of the room.

"How about that drink now?"

You reconsider. "I really shouldn't." You're pretty damn sure that any alcohol at this point would be a mistake. This whole thing is just turning out too weird and you don't want to lose what little sense you have left.

"Oh c'mon, pansy. It's one little drinky-poo."

"No seriously, I'm ok," you respond a little more forcefully.

"Ok, suit yourself." Helen walks over to the desk by the right wall and opens a big drawer, pulling out a non-descript bottle of brown liquor. She also pulls out two rounded glasses and places them on the desktop. *Thoink!* The cork of the bottle comes off. Ignoring your previous protests, Helen fills both glasses about one-third full. She picks up her glass and takes a sip, savoring the liquor, eyes closed.

Helen opens her eyes and looks at you. "See, not poisoned my fearful fuck buddy. Sure you don't want that drink before we get started exploring our bodies?"

You hate being called a "pansy", and it clearly isn't poisonous. *Oh, what the fuck.* You step over and pick up your glass, swirling and sniffing the brown liquor. It has an herbal smell to it with overtones of cinnamon.

"What is it?" you ask, your nose still taking in the delightful aroma.

"It's Ukrainian. I got it from a monastery there a few months back when I was travelling in the area. They brew it onsite. It's phenomenal stuff, quite tasty and unique. They don't distribute it at all, hence the plain bottle you saw me pour from. Go on, have a drink. You'll love it, I guarantee."

You toss your head back and let the shot course down your throat. It has an odd, sweet taste to it and no burn, a telling characteristic of better grade liquor. You close your eyes, reveling in the taste. *This shit is pretty tight!*

You open your eyes and notice that the lights are brighter somehow, and you have to squint to keep your eyes from closing instinctively. You also notice that you are starting to feel a little light-headed. *Damn,* you think, *that was some powerful stuff!*

You go to set your cup back down only to find it's a bit difficult to see the desk. Everything is getting kinda fuzzy while continuing to grow brighter. You have to angle one hand over your eyes to keep them open. Growing fearful, you drop your glass which shatters on the floor. Through squinted eyes you look over at Helen. She glows brightest of all, her outline blurring, taking on an elongated shape with large eyes and a bulbous head.

"What the fuck is happening to me?!" you yell out, panicked. "What the hell did you give me to drink?" You start flailing around, not sure where you're going but knowing that you need to get out of here.

The responding voice is low and soothing. "Don't fight it, earth man. We've picked you to be a subject in our research. We think that as a representation of your species you will be very enlightening to some unanswered questions we have."

We? Who's "we"? You take a step forward and find your legs no longer support your weight. You crumple to the floor, and the darkness closes in where the light used to be.

*　　*　　*　　*

You wake up four days later in Dachedong Village, Hunan province, China. Your ass really hurts.

The End

"Uh…Turn left!" you scream.

"Where does that go?" asks Loretta hurriedly.

"I don't know exactly, but turn left, goddammit! We sure as shit don't want to head farther into the city!"

With squealing tires, the car sweeps through the intersection, the tail end flying out, fishtailing wildly.

"Step on it," you wail. "We need to gain some distance. I figure we can lose them in the burbs just outside of town. Growing up, I used to play a game of Hide and Seek there with my friends in our cars. Trust me. This will work." Loretta simply answers with a doubtful sound and concentrates on redlining her poor, little four cylinder car.

The two of you fly away from downtown proper; buildings give way to strip malls. You're starting to sweat bullets wondering if these douche nozzles following you will be as dim-witted as some of your friends whom you could easily ditch back in the day. You look over at Loretta who is not faring much better and looks equally, if not more, tense than you.

"Hey, I'm sorry about all this," you try to apologize. "I honestly didn't think that this would happen. I mean, I figured you were kidding when you said that guy had friends who would kick my ass."

"Uh… certainly NOT kidding. Listen honey, you're cute, but I kinda made a bad decision. I really shouldn't have let you two fight over me. I just got so wrapped up in the moment. God, I'm so goddamn stupid sometimes. What was I thinking? You know, if those country bumpkins back there find out who I really am, I have no doubt that I'm going to share the same beatdown as you."

Confused, you look at Loretta, trying to make sense of what she just said. "What? What do you mean...who you 'really' are? Who are... HOLY SHIT! LOOK OUT! CAR!"

Immediately ahead, a car to your right is hauling ass toward the intersection. Unfortunately, they have the green light and are expecting you to stop. You only have a split second to react.

Scream "Turn turn turn!"
Turn to page 138

Scream "Speed up! You can make it!"
Turn to page 182

You look at Sofia, smiling.

"Hell yeah. Let's go! I'll call my boss and tell 'em that I've got chicken pox and will be gone for a while. Or shit, I'll say I have mono! That'll buy me plenty of time."

"I have no idea what craziness you are talking about," Sofia responds.

"It doesn't matter. Let's get tickets. Point the way!"

Sofia directs you toward an airline counter and the two of you make your way over. There is hardly any line with the lateness of the hour, and you wait only a second to book your flight.

"Two tickets to Brazil for tonight, please," you ask.

"Rio de Janeiro," Sofia chimes in after you, smiling at your rather broad destination request.

"That flight is a little full. The best I can do is seats 13A and 13B. With airport taxes and fees, the total comes to $1034.78. How would you like to pay for that?"

You balk a little since you're not sure if you have that much room left on your VISA. It's going to be close. You reach into your back pocket and pull out your worn, black leather wallet.

"Is there room in First Class?" Sofia inquires.

"Let me check," the airline employee replies.

"Uh… I don't think we need First Class, do we? I mean, we're just going to sleep, right?" You panic thinking how much more this trip is going to cost if you travel First Class.

"Yes, we can accommodate you in First Class. I have seats 4C and 4D. Flying first class, you ticket price will be $5403.65." Your eyes open wide and your mouth goes dry. *Holy shit!* There's <u>no way</u> you can pay for that. *Fuck, that's even way above my credit limit!* Your pulse quickens and you feel like an ass having to tell Sofia that you're too poor to accompany her. She's probably going to dismiss you like a dyslexic at a reading competition.

"That'll be fine," Sofia says calmly as she opens her clutch and pulls out a platinum credit card.

plane. You peek out into the darkened aircraft, and it seems as though everyone slept through your exploits. You breathe a huge sigh of relief.

With Sofia's hand in yours, the two of you make your way back to your seats. As you settle in and close your eyes, you have no idea what's in store for you when the plane lands, but at this point... who cares.

The End

Seriously scraped up with large swaths of skin etched by flakes of blood, you are taken to jail and brought before the booking sergeant. Thank God, at least now you're wearing clothing again, albeit in the form of an ill-fitting orange jumpsuit.

"Sir," you start, "I can explain. I know this must seem strange to you, but there is an explanation, honest. I have a good reason for all of this."

"Oh, I'm sure," the sergeant replies matter-of-factly. He looks up from your paperwork with dubious eyes. "Well, go ahead sir, but realize anything you say can and will be held against you in a court of law."

"Fine. Whatever," you respond, desperation rising in your voice. "You gotta believe I sure as hell didn't mean to be naked in a public library. See, I met this chick– actually, I went out with this other chick Brandi, a friend of mine, to a piano bar. It was Hook and Swagger. So, we're drinking and partying and then like I meet this girl, Lille. Very hot, lots of fun. And then 'Respect' comes on, you know, the song by Aretha Franklin, and I'm all dancing and singing and well, things happen and I had to leave." You stammer a little at the end there trying to gloss over the fact you gave one of the bodyguards a bloody nose and got thrown out.

"So this somehow leads to you being naked in an underground archive, I take it?" the sarge asks with raised eyebrows, a hint of a smile playing on his lips.

"No. I mean, yes. But not directly. So like, I go to Rudy's diner down the block and have some pie and coffee."

"And the pie made you want to take off your clothes?"

"No!" you protest, knowing that the sergeant is starting to fuck with you. "I met this girl there named Sam, I mean Samantha, and she tricked me into going to the library."

"Tricked you?"

"Yeah. That bitch said that she worked in the archives and wanted to show me some old maps or something. But get this: She takes me down there, fucks me and then like runs off with all my clothes, leaving me trapped in this goddamn maze of books and shit three floors down. What the hell, right?!"

"Right," the sergeant agrees dubiously. "She fucked you and then managed to steal all your clothes while you what... read a good book?"

"No, I was still drunk, that's why I didn't drive there in the first place. I mean, with my car, the car I took to the bar. I mean... God! Come on! I get points for that, right? Not drinking and driving?

"So anyway, I fell asleep after she fucked me. I must've still been drunk, I guess, or something. OR, maybe yet, she slipped something into my pie! I bet that's what happened!"

"Doped the pie, huh? Gotcha. Yup, we get that a lot around here. Vicious bitches doping baked goods in order to swindle clothes off unsuspecting victims. I feel your pain, sir. But listen, we all have jobs to do and mine right now is to book your ass for trespassing and indecent exposure. Sorry friend."

You begin to protest but realize you already sound like some crazy asshole, and you're only going to dig yourself in deeper if you continue. Throughout the morning and the rest of the day, you are moved from one holding cell to another; until finally, you are put into a cell with bunk beds to spend the night until your roommate can bail you out in the morning.

Soon after you're deposited in your cell, another prisoner is escorted to join you. It's explained that Bobby, six foot five and well over four hundred pounds, is to be your cellmate for the night. *Great,* you think, *fat prisoner in a little cell. This is going to be interesting. I bet he was caught shoplifting candy bars, the fat fuck. Dude could* <u>*definitely*</u> *put away the candy bars,* you note with a smile. *Uh oh, what if he wants the top bunk? That fat fucker could crush me to death if the bolts give!*

"Hey, uh... Bobby. How's it going? Um. Just thinking about it... uh, mind if I sleep on top? I mean, the top bunk?"

You laugh nervously, wondering how gay jokes go over in prison.

Unfortunately, the next few hours teach you that gay jokes actually don't go over all that well. Turns out that Bobby (who is not in for shoplifting but for vehicular homicide) has a thing for cute little guys like yourself and decides to teach you the intricate ways of prison courting and inevitable manlove.

Maybe you will be getting lucky on this adventure after all.

The End

You figure your chances at getting back in are slim to none and if Lille saw the scene you made on your way out, there's probably no chance in Hell she's gonna want to see you again. You sigh. *Oh well.* Mind made up, you start walking toward Rudy's All-Night Kitchen, a shiny steel-clad establishment a ways down the block.

Rudy's has always been a great go-to destination when late night coffee and pie are in order. Moreover, given the difficulty you have walking in any fashion that remotely approximates a straight line, coffee and pie tonight are a must.

The door jingles as you enter the diner. You meander to the counter and plunk yourself down on a stool. You lower your head onto your arms and close your eyes, trying to keep the diner from spinning too violently around you. Within seconds, a friendly old voice greets you as if you were kin.

"What'll it be son?" the voice asks. You look up at Rudy standing behind the counter and have a hard time keeping him from drifting out of your vision. His white apron and pointy hat seem very bright in the fluorescent light.

"Black coffee. Cherry pie. No ice cream." You close your eyes and put your head back down on the counter.

"Coming right up." Another jingle sounds somewhere far off. A haze is settling in on your brain. You can feel yourself starting to fall asleep.

"Big night there, Sinatra?" a pleasant female voice asks.

You raise your head and weakly glance over. Sitting next to you is a conservatively dressed woman in her mid-twenties, her hair worn up on her head, held in place by a yellow pencil. She's smiling at you, her blue eyes sparkling with humor behind her glasses.

"As a matter of fact, yup." You put your head back down. The woman next to you orders a slice of pie and a glass of water.

Soon both of your orders arrive, so once again you begrudgingly rouse yourself to the world.

"Here, this is for you," the woman says as she pushes the big glass of water in front of you. You smile wanly at her and take the water, drinking it all at once. Rehydrated, you start feeling a little bit better.

"Don't they just have the best pie here?" the woman remarks.

You take a big pull on your cup of joe then look over at her. "Yes. Yes they do." You smile and introduce yourself. She introduces herself as Sam, short for Samantha. The two of you talk, intermittently at first as you try to shake off the night's activities thus far and sober up a little. After a while, the two of you are chatting animatedly.

Pie long gone and three cups of coffee later, you're feeling much better. Suddenly, it occurs to you that you have no idea what Sam does for a living so you ask.

"Why I'm a librarian. I've always loved books– the smell of the paper, the feeling of the printed page between my fingers. I especially love old books. I'm really lucky that most of my work at the library is in the basement archives. It's a labyrinth of knowledge going back hundreds of years about every conceivable topic. To know that the authors all around you have turned to dust while their thoughts persevere..." She shutters playfully and giggles softly to herself. "I'm such a dork."

It all makes sense now: the conservative clothes, the dowdy appearance, the erudite conversation (mostly on her end), the number two pencil in her hair. *God, she's cute*, you think to yourself. You've always had a sexy librarian fantasy and man, is she hitting every button.

"Hey, it's– wow! It's almost five a.m. Wanna get out of here?" you ask, inwardly praying that she'll say "yes".

"Hmmm... I don't usually go out with strangers I meet at the diner, but you ARE very well dressed," she responds with hesitation. Then suddenly more lively she continues, "You know, I don't have to be back at the library until four p.m. for my shift, so sure. Let's hang out. In fact, I'd love to show you the stacks at the library if you're interested. It'd just be us until the morning crew arrives in a few hours."

Oh sweet Jesus, is she reading my mind? Although, as fun as the sexy librarian fantasy might be, getting her to come back to your place may be more of a sure thing. Hmmmm… that's a hard decision.

———————————————

Do you hit the stacks at the library?
Turn to page 48

Do you suggest your house instead?
Turn to page 45

You arrive at the Landing Strip, a single story building with large floor-to-ceiling windows revealing a dimly lit, elegant interior. A huge bronze statue of a crashed bi-plane stands just outside the opening to the club– an obvious testament to the poor shmoes that crash and burn at this place nightly, never setting sight upon its female namesake. You step inside.

The club's décor exudes a chic styling with plenty of warm touches. Indirect lighting casts an orange glow on birch-paneled walls, setting an intimate mood. Many of the walls have beautiful inlaid patterns of cherry and mahogany giving the club an updated speakeasy feel. A jazz quartet fills the club with music from a small stage at the front. The stage is encircled by small round tables, all heavily populated. Since you and Pete didn't get a reservation, the two of you are relegated to a bar area in the back that is mostly standing room only.

You stay behind to stake out a place and send Pete to the bar to get drinks for both of you. He returns with two glasses of his current drink-de-jour, the Rusty Nail. One sip tells you that this drink will easily become a favorite since it's strong and goes down smooth. After your third helping, your confidence at an all-time drunken high, you decide it's time to make your move on the indigenous female prey.

Throughout the night, idly chatting with Pete about forgettable subjects, you have been sizing up the bar patrons, deciding which are worthy of your time. At the moment, you notice that not one, but two, lovely ladies are at the bar chatting with friends. You hope their conversations are not terribly important since it's time to interrupt someone. With purpose and vigor you stride confidently to the bar, standing betwixt the two in your sights. You order your fourth Rusty Nail, a bit loudly to see if either notices your drink order. They don't.

To your right stands a tall, dark, sultry brunette, her hair a deep chocolate brown. She has prominent Nordic facial features and speaks what you guess to be Bulgarian. It's a guttural language and not at all becoming on the fair lips that utter such words. You can't help but admire her long legs, made even more noteworthy by thigh-high, black leather riding boots ending precious inches beneath a short-cut skirt. The soft, creamy skin exposed between boots and skirt provides an overwhelming temptation to run your hand up it slowly to the promised land above.

On the other hand, to your left is a smaller woman with dark espresso colored hair that flows like water around her shoulders. A bright pink hibiscus blossom sits perched among her sea of mahogany tresses and compliments the South of the Border feel of her dress. Her mocha-colored skin glows warmly in the orange lighting of the club on limbs that glide gracefully through the air when she moves. Unlike the other woman, this woman is talking in English but with a thick Spanish accent.

You're faced with a choice that men everywhere dream about. Do you choose North or South?

———————————————

Hit on the Bulgarian chick.
Turn to page 277

Hit on the Spanish chick.
Turn to page 5

"Pardon me," you loudly interrupt the Bulgarian woman in the middle of her conversation, enunciating your words as if she is both deaf and slightly stupid, "but I couldn't help overhearing you."

The woman stops and looks at you with a puzzled expression, as does the woman she's conversing with- a blonde woman, clearly Dutch or Norwegian from her tall, slender build. You notice both women are very muscular, their toned arms well defined in the dim light.

"tlhIngan Hol Dajatlh'e'?" the Bulgarian woman asks you.

"Uh... what?"

"Sorry. Just checking." the Bulgarian says in clear English with a tinge of an accent.

"Oh my God, your English is AMAZING!"

"Thanks, I learned it in Madison."

"Is that in Bulgaria?" you ask.

"Um... no. It's in Wisconsin- you know, Great Lakes, cheese, etc."

"Oh, I didn't realize you had studied there. Does your friend speak English?"

"Oh no. She doesn't speak a word." The Bulgarian smiles and looks at her friend who just shakes her head "no" and shrugs. The Bulgarian woman then points to you saying, "yIntagh" and the two of them snicker. You feel a little like an outsider as you are not privy to their inside joke.

To cover your growing insecurity, you hastily ask if they would like another glass of what appears to be wine.

"Sure. That sounds great! Two more Blood Wines." *Hmmm... must be some sort of cabernet or merlot thing. Maybe like a sangria? Whatever.* You flag the barkeep over and order up two glasses of 'Blood Wine'. He looks at you with a curiously pathetic look, shakes his head and rolls his eyes. Soon however, he's back with two ceramic mugs of a deep red liquid that you pay for.

"Here you go ladies! Bottoms up! So what brings you to this neck of the woods?" The Bulgarian woman responds that they are in town attending a conference for a few days. *Ugh, booooooring. Conferences tend to blow ass.* You switch the subject.

After a few minutes of talking, you signal Pete to come over. When he arrives, you try your best to send him some subtle, non-verbal signals to lure the Dutch chick away from your Bulgarian prey. Having had a number of drinks during the night as well, he's a bit slow on the uptake and your attempts meet with abject failure.

You, Pete and the Bulgarian drink and talk for a while— the Dutch woman laughing along when she sees the three of you laugh. She's clearly shy and out of her element with the three of you prattling on in English. After a number of rounds of drinks, you start feeling bad for 'Dutchy' and decide to include her. Slowly and loudly you ask, "WHAT DO YOU DO FOR A LIVING?" mimicking digging and typing, the first two jobs that come to mind.

The Bulgarian responds, slightly slurring her s's at this point, "She's not deaf, remember? She just doesn't speak English, ya *p'tahk.*" You sheepishly apologize for having forgotten that in your drunken haze. "Actually we're both students of combat and D'Har." Pete nudges you.

"Really? Hmmm. So what, are you in the Army or something?"

"Not quite. What we practice is called '*moQ'bara*'. There's a lot of hand-to-hand combat and fighting with a *bat'letH*. It's great for getting your adrenaline pumping and driving blood lust into a fervor. For the mind, we use the D'Har to focus our abilities and enhance our training."

"Wicked! I'd love to see some moves, if you're down to show me. Just don't hurt me, K?" you smile and wink. Pete nudges you again but you ignore him.

"Well, we're staying up the street at the Radisson. We could all walk there if you think you can make it. In fact, maybe if you're lucky you can both be *par'machpu'* by morning." She winks at you seductively. You're not sure what it means to be a *par'machpu'*, but it certainly sounds pretty damn good. She continues adding, "We leave tomorrow, so tonight's our last night here."

Oh hell yeah, you think. *This is going to be perfect! One night and then BOOM, no long term commitment even possible. Pete's the fuckin' man for suggesting this place!*

You reply, "Excellent! And don't worry about me, I'm not too drunk to walk, not yet at least! What do you think ladies, shall we leave?" Pete nudges you again, this time pretty hard. You look over at him sorta pissed. You lean in to make sure the ladies can't overhear you.

"What the fuck, dude! We've got these honeys ready to roll, what gives?"

"Listen, I need to tell ya something but not here. Can you meet me in the bathroom in a few minutes?"

"Hey bro, I'm not going to fuckin' go pee-pees with you like a couple of chicks. Tell me what you gotta tell me," you insist.

"No, it can't be here."

"Are we going or are you going to be a little *bIHnuch?*" the Bulgarian asks, seemingly ready to leave.

Find out what the hell has Pete's panties all in a bunch?
Turn to page 280

Time to get it on at the hotel!
Turn to page 93

"Alright dude," you tell Pete in a forceful whisper. "This better be fuckin' worth it. I'll meet you in the bathroom in a few minutes." Pete makes an excuse that he has to use the john before you guys leave. You talk a little more with the women, shooting the shit, until a few minutes have passed and then mention that you should hit the head too. The women take no note in the fact that both of you have gone to the bathroom and start conversing again in their native guttural language.

You make your way to the men's room and angrily push open the door. Pete looks up from the sink where he's splashing some water on his face. Water drips down his nose and small drops are caught on his eyebrows.

"Ok. What the fuck. I've single-handedly lined up foreign pussy for both of us, and you wanna mess with a sure thing for what? What's so goddamn important that you have to pull us away from the best one night stand we're ever gonna to have?"

Pete pulls out a paper towel from the nearby dispenser, dries his face and then looks at you with a matter-of-fact expression. "So douchebag, any idea what language they're speaking?"

"Sounds like Bulgarian or some eastern European thing. Why?"

"That's what I thought, dumbass. It's not Bulgarian, Estonian, Polish or Czech. It's fuckin' Klingon. Those women are here for the big sci-fi conference that just wrapped. Judging from their Blood Wine, their obvious hulkin' build, and their mastery of the Klingon language, those chicks are full on freaks, dude. You should stay the hell away from them. They're gonna fuckin' beat the shit out of you if you go back with them."

You pause, not so sure any more about these girls. To kill time while you make up your mind, you walk over to the sink and idly wash your hands. After a minute or so, you turn off the water, and with wet hands, slick back your hair. You place both hands on the sides of the sink and look hard at yourself in the mirror, contemplating the possible outcomes ahead. You stand up, dry your hands on your pants, turn to Pete and say…

Fuck this. Let's get the hell outta here!
Turn to page 179

Let's tame these Klingon bitches!
Turn to page 93

"Holy shit! Holy FUCKING shit!" you exclaim. "I kicked some dude's ass to be with another dude?! Fuck me! Oh my God, Oh my God. Listen Loren," you say, "uh... um... I just gotta... uh... yeah." You open the door and get out. You walk to the back of the car, your thoughts a jumble, not totally sure what just happened.

Ok, calm down, you tell yourself. *Breathe. In (pause) then out. In and out.* Your mind is racing. You rationalize that you can just call a cab. That's right. You can call a cab and run out at the last second to catch it. It'd work. Even if the douchebags in the pickup trucks are waiting, you should be able to make it to the cab and pay the cabbie whatever he wants to lose them. *That could totally work,* you decide. You reach into your pocket and pull out your cell.

Loren rolls down the window and leans out awkwardly. "Listen, I'm sorry I kinda sprung this on you. You were just so cute! And then when you beat up Teddy, I just thought..." Loren sighs. "I'm sorry you're having trouble with who I am, but please, get back in the car and we'll figure out what to do. Please?"

You look at Loren, his face one step removed from a crying Tammy Faye Bakker circa 1987. His baleful eyes plead for acceptance. You look down at your cell phone.

Suck it up and get back in the car.
Turn to page 309

Tell Loren you've got it handled and no thanks.
Turn to page 98

"Oh Jesus Christ. Kitty, you can <u>not</u> use the cat for foreplay! It fuckin' hurts, and it's creepier than shit."

Dejected, Kitty puts down Chairman Meow and pouts at you. "I thought you'd like it."

You roll over onto your back underneath Kitty so that she is now straddling the General, who doesn't seem concerned at all about giving away his position.

"Forget the cat. It's not a big deal. Now get down here and kiss me you minx," you say, being purposeful with your pet name for her. Kitty splashes down on top of you, her breasts mushing into your chest as the two of you kiss passionately. You take this opportunity to awkwardly pull down your underwear to your ankles where you flick 'em off onto the floor. You then move Kitty's g-string aside and penetrate her deeply. She groans in ecstatic satisfaction.

The two of you fuck hard and heavy, Kitty moaning loudly. She's dripping wet which makes the sex easy and fun. Occasionally, the woman reverts to her sexy, angry cat noises which are a bit off-putting, but you choose to ignore them and focus on the task at hand.

You roll Kitty over and push her legs up, entering her again in a missionary variation. Faster and faster you pump Kitty, savoring each thrust, almost fully removing your cock before punching it back in. *Oh yeah, regardless of all her craziness, this chick knows how to fuck!*

Rarrrrrhhhh, SWIPE! Four outstretched daggers lash out at your swinging ball sack and the pain tears through you. Hissler has clearly decided that your nutsack is a fascinating play toy, much better than that crappy catnip mouse he left under the couch.

You scream out instinctually and without thinking, turn and take a forceful swing at the cat, unable to contain your primal, sex-driven rage. Your reaction catches the playful cat off guard and connects fully, sending Hissler flying off the bed. Kitty cries out seeing you hit her baby and pushes you off of her.

Der Furrer hits the floor with a dead thunk and lays there... still. Uncaring about the cat, you check your sack to see if there is any blood coming out of it and just what damage that fucking animal did to your nuts.

Kitty meanwhile, dashes over to her prone cat and leans down to listen for a heartbeat.

"That fucking cat took a chunk out of my nutsack! Goddammit! What the fuck is going on here?!" you say, completely unsympathetic to the cat you just slugged.

Kitty looks back at you, tears coursing down her face, her eyes bloodshot. "You killed him! You killed Hissler! You son of a bitch!"

"Well, I'm sure he deserved it from the millions of Jew mice he murdered," you respond, not really sure why you're making a joke in such bad taste at such a bad time. Fury grips Kitty's face, and you can see her gnash her teeth in anger.

Suddenly, Kitty reaches over to the bookshelf less than an arm's length away and grabs a book. She hunkers back onto her knees and flings it at you, missing you completely.

"Fuck you! Fuck you, you cat killer! Burn in hell!" She reaches over, grabs another book and throws it at you, this time coming a bit closer. She throws like a girl, so you're not all that concerned.

"Hey, I'm sorry. I'm really sorry. But your fuckin' cat ripped into my balls. I didn't mean to hit him. It was just a reaction. I couldn't help it," you try to rationalize to Kitty. She's not buying it.

Kitty grabs another book, spilling a few more on to the carpet. She hauls back and throws it. This time, the book connects with your face and smashes into your nose, causing your eyes to well up with tears and a thin trickle of blood to creep out of your nose.

"Stop throwing books at me, you bitch. If you didn't have all those fucking cats, none of this would have happened!" You're super pissed off, and you quickly reach down to retrieve your underwear, all the while keeping an eye trained on Kitty and her arsenal of books. Another book flies by your head, and you dodge to the side.

"My fault? My fault! That's it." Kitty lurches over and pushes the rest of the numerous books off the shelf, scattering them across the floor below. Hidden behind the books is a double barrel shotgun.

"Oh fuck!" you yell and leap up, underwear in hand. You bound past Kitty who is withdrawing the weapon from the shelf. You race down the hallway to the sounds of Kitty yelling and the definitive cock of a double barrel shotgun. You grab your clothes and head for the front door. Panicked, you throw your head around to see how close Kitty is with her gun.

When you turn back around, you enter full steam into the entangling net of the sand orb mobile. Thin nylon strands weave their way around your arms and into the clothes that you are carrying, causing you to stop, momentarily ensnared. You give the whole thing a big jerk toward the floor, freeing yourself. Unfortunately, your entrapment costs you valuable time.

You reach for the door handle, one twist away from freedom.

"Fuck you cat killer!"

A deafening explosion erupts behind you and shotgun pellets cleave through your naked back. The force of the blast slams you into the closed door and you bounce off, falling onto the hamburger meat which once was your back. The pain is unbearable, and you can feel yourself losing consciousness.

Kitty walks over, shotgun dangling from one hand. She kneels by your head. Her hazy figure undulates in your teary vision.

Kitty bends down next to you. In a soft voice laced with hate, she whispers in your ear.

"I'll see you in Hell."

With both hands, Kitty brings the shotgun up over her head and slams it down onto your throat, crushing your windpipe. You gasp weakly for the smallest iota of air which never comes. Your eyes flutter closed, your last vision of life being the crazed face of Kitty, smirking over you as you asphyxiate.

Realizing you're dead, Kitty places the shotgun on the ground next to you and goes into the kitchen to get a sharp butcher's knife. Over the next few weeks you make a marvelous meal for her remaining four kitties.

The End

"MMMMmmmm..." you eye her up and down. "I hope you're taking your calcium, cuz I don't want you to break a hip later tonight," you say in your most sensuously deep voice.

She pauses, momentarily struck by your approach. The smile fades into a contemplative stare. "Really?" she says. "That's the best you got at 1:30 a.m.?"

You look down, a bit embarrassed with yourself for saying something like that to a woman old enough to be your mother. She laughs riotously seeing your discomfiture.

"I'm just fuckin' with you, young man. Well, step back a tic and let me have a look at you." She cases your features from head to toe, pausing uncomfortably long at your crotch. "You look nice enough. Ya got a good thing goin' on with the suit. So, if I might ask then, what happened with the blonde back there– the one who pantomimed throwing her drink on you?"

"Oh her? She was a real loon, I think kinda psycho. I don't go for that. Dated one in high school. When we split, bitch cut the stems on all four of my tires– even forced opened the trunk and slashed the spare! I guess it was no surprise, really, since she was a cutter. She carved my name into her forearm, for Chrissake. Freaky ass shit, man. So, no thanks, no more crazies for me."

"Good call on your part," she remarks.

With seemingly nothing else to say, the woman turns, picks up and drains the remainder of her drink, returning the glass to the bar with a satisfied sound– all in one fluid motion. The last call bell rings out, and she signals the bartender for another.

You're not sure what to say at this point. You kinda blew it with your opening, and any cougar worth her salt is going to see through any further lame convo. You take a sip of your martini as she rattles the ice left in her empty glass, watching the bartender make her drink. An uncomfortable silence ensues. You glance around absentmindedly, debating whether to just give up and go home.

Finally, it's the woman who breaks the silence by coughing politely to get your attention.

"So, let me throw a proposition to you at this late hour," she says. "As we both know, you clearly have no better prospects tonight. What say you let me make you a real man?" She raises her eyebrows with a smirk painted across her face. "Judging from what I've seen, I suspect you've got a lot to learn in pleasing a woman sexually." Her drink arrives.

Screw you, no woman leaves MY bed disappointed!
Turn to page 82

School me, Mistress Barfly.
Turn to page 46

You smile at Helen. You've always wanted to do this. It's a bit of a personal fantasy and even more, a secret *Fuck You* to the owner.

"How about we go to the café I work at?" you suggest to Helen. "Ok with that?"

"Fuck if I care," Helen responds with an intoxicated slur.

"Cool." You turn to the driver. "We're going to the Coffee Haus on Twelfth and Kinnyson."

As the cab pulls away from the curb, you turn back to Helen. "God, it's kinda a lame name for the place, huh? The owner is a real prick with no imagination. Oh, I'll just call it 'Haus' instead of 'House'," you say, spelling out each word in the owner's voice with a mocking tone. "Sooooo fuckin' original." Helen rolls her eyes and smiles in agreement. She puts her hand on your knee.

You lean back against the seat, your head swimming in booze. You close your eyes for a second, feeling the bounce of the cab over the city streets. *This is going to be great,* you think. *We're going to fuck on the owner's desk and in his big, fuckin' black pleather chair. Maybe I'll even cream in the half-n-half jug.* You smile.

Suddenly, you feel Helen's hand move slowly from your knee toward your belt– a tender touch following the seam of your pants in, then up your fly. You open your eyes and look over inquisitively at her. She smiles a broad smile and her eyebrows flicker playfully as her hand dips down between your pants and your waist.

Slowly, Helen starts to stroke your manhood. Beginning with the rhythm of the car, the pace of her hand moves quicker and quicker as your cab ride continues. *Oh my GOD, being in the hands of an experienced woman is better than any of those other chicks!* You shut your eyes again, enjoying the sensation. A little moan escapes your lips as you feel yourself building to a climax. Unnoticed by either of you, the driver's eyes appear in the rear view mirror in response to your sounds of pleasure.

Suddenly, without warning, the taxi slams on its brakes sending you flying into the Plexiglas that separates you from the driver. You turn your face at the last second, and your cheekbone hits the surface hard, rattling your teeth. Helen yelps out in pain– her wrist twisting unnaturally in your pants as you're cast forward. You groan as you push yourself back from the glass.

"The FUCK you're gonna bust a nut in my cab!" the driver screams at you, his Indian accent much more pronounced now. "Get the fuck out, the two of you! Goddamn Harold and Maude fucking in the back of my cab? Oh no, I don't think so." The two of you exit sheepishly from the cab before it speeds off, a parting finger erupting from the driver's window.

You look around to get your bearings. *Whew.* Thank God, you're only blocks from where you work.

"So, wanna walk the rest of the way to the coffee shop?" you ask. "It's only a few blocks from here. Then we could... pick up where we left off?" You smile at her, winking suggestively. She looks at you, rubbing her injured wrist, the spark in her eyes exchanged for apologetic weariness.

"Nah, I'm sorry kid. Not this time. I'm getting too old for this shit. I'm just going to call another taxi and head home. I think you're gonna have to take care of that yourself tonight," she says, pointing at your crotch. You stare at her, crestfallen.

"But...," you plead.

"Like I said, sorry," Helen says with a remorseful face. "Night kid." She turns to leave. After a few steps, she pauses then looks back at you.

"And stay away from the self-tanner," she adds with a half-smile. You close your eyes and sigh, listening to her high heels click in their staccato rhythm as she walks away.

The End

"I don't know why I'm telling you this…" you blurt out getting her attention, "but this one time in middle school I accidently grabbed self-tanner to jack off with. For a week my dick looked like one of those hopeless wienies turning forever on the rollers at a 7-11 gas station."

Silence. *Oh God,* you think, *does she think I'm funny or just a freak?* You look wistfully at her and notice the corners of her mouth start to curl up. A moment later she bursts out laughing hysterically.

"Oh my God, that's hilarious!" Helen manages to get out between laughs, tears rolling down her cheeks. *Whew,* you inwardly sigh. *Ice broken.* After a few minutes of laughing, she calms down and uses her cocktail napkin to dab at the corners of her eyes.

She looks at you, a much different emotion in her eyes now.

"Hell of a conversation starter you got there," Helen leads off, beginning a night of easy conversation. The two of you talk animatedly, drinking frequently, both managing to squeeze in another round before last call. You continue to share embarrassing stories with Helen, both of you laughing hysterically at your youthful mistakes. It feels great to have someone sharing your ridiculous moments so whole-heartedly.

When the last call bell does ring, you both do a shot of Jäger– a toast to the idiotic moments in life.

In an attempt to sober up slightly before leaving, over time and water you start to learn more about Helen and what brings her here. Never married, career-oriented, Helen has clearly traveled quite a bit in life. Her stories of the Far East keep you enthralled until the two of you are asked politely, yet firmly, to leave. You look around and sure enough, the entire place is a ghost town. The bar officially closed quite a while ago.

You gulp down the remains of your water and realize that your cheekbones hurt from smiling so much. Damn, you're SO glad you met Helen. She's the real deal, and it seems as though the two of you have really hit it off. Now, for the closer. How are you going to propose spending the night together?

As the two of you make your way to the exit, you glimpse at Helen, her face glowing from the fun you've been having. Being a gentleman, you hold the door open for her. As she passes by, she pauses and suddenly kisses you. The two of you make out passionately in the bar's entryway, kissing like the sloppy drunks you are, until the barkeep, completely sickened by your smooching, clears his throat loudly. Helen pulls away, looking in your eyes, and walks out.

Realizing you both are too drunk to drive, you call a cab. It's not long before one shows up, and the two of you pile into the back, laughing.

"Where to?" the driver asks with a slight Indian accent. Helen looks to you inquisitively.

You suggest a place.
Turn to page 289

Let Helen make the call.
Turn to page 233

"I'm sorry, Dixie," you apologize. "I'm not the spanking type. This whole 'bad little girl' thing really isn't working for me."

Dixie harumphs, her face pouting at your unwillingness to play along.

"Oh alright, fine!" she says disappointed and sits down on the couch next to you. "I might as well tell you the rest of the story then." Dixie crosses her legs, bringing her tat into view.

"Margie honey, do you wanna come in here?" Dixie calls out. You hear a door creak open and from the hallway emerges one of the burliest women you have ever seen. Tattoos cover both arms, portraying a number of scenes, words and symbology. The largest tattoo, prominently encasing most of Margie's mammoth right bicep, is a bloody heart stabbed through with a sword. From the sword a banner flies which encircles the heart– the name 'Dixie' in Olde English script emblazoned across it. *Oh shit,* you think. *These two have some sort of prison love connection!*

Dixie continues, "So when I went to prison, Margie here took me under her wing and kept me safe. She was my brilliant knight in shiny armor during one of the worst times in my life." You look over at Margie who stands quietly at the hallway entrance, silent, stern and certainly imposing. Smiling, Dixie gets up and glides over to the large woman, looking lovingly at her the entire time. At her side, Dixie slowly traces out the heart on the she-beast's arm with a caring touch. "You see, my little Margie was in prison for what she did to this very bad trucker who hurt her."

"Bashed his fuckin' skull in with a tire iron is what I did," Margie blurts out, her husky voice dripping with residual anger. "Nobody takes Marge for a fool. Motherfucker was makin' advances I didn't like."

Marge looks down at Dixie and puts one arm tenderly around her, covering her shoulders like a thick scarf. She then shifts her countenance to you, her eyes burning with a general hate. *Ohhh my God,* you think, your eyes growing wide with fear. *Dixie is Margie's prison bitch and here I am– caught in the living room, mostly naked, trying to fuck her! This cannot end well.*

"So, what do you think of that, pretty boy?" Marge asks menacingly.

What do I think? I think I need to get the FUCK out of here! you answer wordlessly.

———————

Try to leave politely.
Turn to page 295

Run!
Turn to page 109

You stand up, shirt spilling open, your tie dangling stupidly atop your bare chest. You have to hold up your pants to keep them from falling.

"Well, um… that was a… uh… um… a very tragic tale, Margie," you say as sympathetic as you can without overdoing it.

"Name's 'Marge' to you, motherfucker! Only Dixie can call me that."

"Oh yes, um… Marge, of course. Well, it's plain to me you were clearly wronged, and that trucker guy had just what was coming to him. Anyway… whew! Look at the time! I really should be leaving as I didn't mean to uh… stay quite so late. Wow! It's really late."

All the while you babble, you attempt to dress yourself. You zip up your pants and try to close your shirt by tucking it in and overlapping the buttonless flaps. You pick up your suit coat from the floor and slide your feet into your shoes, pressing down the backs, donning them as slippers for brevity's sake.

"My sincere apologies for taking up your time, and it was very nice to meet you Dixie. Well," you announce, "I guess I'll just be on my way then!"

You shuffle your way awkwardly toward the front door, your shoes flopping underneath, threatening to come off.

Marge breaks away from Dixie and steps in front of you, blocking your path.

"Where the FUCK do you think you're going?" Marge asks, leaning in uncomfortably close, her breath reeking of beer and pork rinds. "My little Dixie wants a manfuck, and she's gonna get it. You better get your sweet little ass back on that couch before I take my fist and show you want it feels like to be a whore in the big house." Your eyes grow wide with the vision of what that would be like. You shutter involuntarily. With great effort, you look past Marge and smile painfully at Dixie, shitting yourself with fear.

Slowly and reluctantly you shuffle back to the couch. You sit down demurely, your hands in your lap, your eyes

"I need to get to High Street near 45th. You have to tell me the way," Loren yells at you, his eyes glued on the road ahead, flowing like a dark swollen river underneath the car. You take note of the street signs as you fly past them to get your bearings. You tell Loren to take a left in three blocks which will be 45th Ave.

Taking the turn way too fast, the Honda swings wide and the tail end whips around hitting the curb. You hear one of the hubcaps wrench free and skitter noisily away. Within minutes of getting on 45th, a pair of headlights joins you.

"They're still behind us and I think they're gaining," Loren updates you.

"Fuck."

You scream through another intersection, narrowly avoiding blinding headlights descending on you from the North. Brakes screech out from the opposing vehicle and Loren swerves instinctually, hardly slowing, nimbly darting just shy of the on-coming bumper. You grab the shitgrip in response to his maneuver while your new dark locks whip around to sting your face. A glance out the window at the vehicle's front end that almost hit you instantly informs you that it's a pickup– the other truck!

Once you're clear of the intersection, the truck from the North swings into pursuit, leading the trailing pickup from the garage. Both pickups are after you again. You curse to yourself and mentally calculate how much further away High Street is. You turn around and look back to gauge how much time you have before the V6 trucks overtake your pathetic riceburner.

It's not going to be long. You rack your brain and knowledge of the area for an advantage.

Out of the passenger window the buildings zip by, their façade broken only by the occasional alley, dark cracks in the sheer face of the cityscape. That's it though, that's your advantage: the alleyways. Your car is much more maneuverable in the tight spaces and narrower to boot, a workable advantage should any dumpsters appear.

You turn to Loren. "The alleys! That's our advantage! Your little car may not have the speed on the open road, but we should be able to make it through the alleys faster than those dickheads behind us. From what I can tell, it looks like the alleys come every few buildings so mark the one you wanna take and turn. The sooner the better!"

Loren simply nods and at the very next alley, he pulls up hard on the e-brake, throwing the steering wheel right—sending the car fishtailing sideways before jetting into the alleyway. Entering the canyon-like walls of the neighboring buildings, Loren slows down, hesitant to come up too fast on something ahead like a random trashcan or a sleeping bum. You turn around to see if the trucks have followed.

"Hold up a sec, Loren. Let's see if they come after us."

Loren stops the Honda and the two of you twist around to look out the back window. Darkness swallows the path behind you, the city street a streak of light in the distance. Time creeps by and tension fills the car. You hold your breath in anticipation of the inevitable trucks giving pursuit. The radio plays quietly, the song barely a muted whisper. Not being able to hold your breath any longer, you let it go in a big sigh.

No sooner has the exhale left your lungs than the first pair of headlights swings into the alley. The brick walls light up from the brilliant halogen headlights and overhead lightbar on the truck. *This must be what meeting St. Peter's going to be like if this doesn't work,* you think to yourself.

The lights on the pickup slowly move forward, the driver clearly unsure if the oversized pickup will fit. The truck comes to a halt.

"Fuckers are too big! Hell yeah!" you rejoice. "They can't follow us!" You laugh out loud and hug Loren you're so happy. The two of you congratulate one another on your plan.

CRASH! The truck that had been hesitating at the mouth of the alley suddenly lurches forward sending up sparks from the extended mirrors. Hundreds of tiny stars fall to the ground as exploding mirror shards from the impact are lit up by the second pickup behind. The metal arms that once held the mirrors scrape noisily on the walls, sending up sparks as they etch their way forward.

"Drive!! Drive!! They're coming! Shit shit shit!" you scream as Loren, one step ahead, surges the car forward. You can't help but watch the monstrosity looming up behind you, safe in the knowledge that the path you're forging is clear for them. Oh God, they are totally going to be on you at any second.

"Deadend! Deadend!" Loren starts yelling. You whip your head back around to see a brick face ahead with two dark choices to be had.

Tell Loren to turn left!
Turn to page 301

Tell Loren to turn right!
Turn to page 134

You turn left as sharply as possible. In the tight quarters, the rear end tags the brick wall violently, sending a shockwave through the car. The impact slings your head into your window, shattering it. You can feel the glass pierce the thick wig and cut deep into your scalp. Your body jerks back to center as Loren accelerates forward.

It's not more than a few seconds until the Honda's high beams illuminate multiple dumpsters set on opposing sides of the alley, effectively blocking the car from going any farther. Loren slams on the brakes. Smoke bathes the headlight beams. He throws his arm around the back of your seat for leverage, turns to look back and shoots toward the juncture in reverse.

You desperately hope that he can zip through the intersection before your pursuers block it, but it's not to be. A few seconds before he's about to enter, the pickup truck roars into view, cutting off any hope.

Loren pulls himself back around and slams the car into first, screaming toward the dumpsters.

"You're not thinking of bashing through are you?" you ask Loren fearfully, worried that this whole chase has maybe gotten the better of his good sense.

"Are fucking crazy?! No! When we stop, get ready to run like hell! Get ready... Go!"

Loren slams on the brakes and the two of you toss off your seatbelts and throw open your doors which smash into the sides of the narrow corridor. You have to get out and close them before you can make your way past. As you throw your door shut, the rear window of the car explodes into pieces as a loud report sounds behind you.

"Holy shit, they're shooting at us!" you scream, trying to capture the reality of a situation that you never thought possible. Another cock of the shotgun echoes in the alley, and you scramble forward toward the safety of the dumpsters ahead.

Another **BOOM** rips through the alleyway and you feel your back explode this time, flesh pulled from bone as the buckshot cleaves through. You are flung forcefully against the dumpster ahead of you. Your face hits the dirty metal, bouncing your body onto your tortured back. When you hit the pavement, your wig falls off and the hibiscus flowers on your dress stretch out their red petals, slowly consuming the garment.

Through ringing ears, you hear footsteps approaching. A thick, country accent breaks the air.

"Lookie here boys, I done shot me a faggot! Thank God, I got my faggot huntin' license this year. Wouldn't wanna be breakin' no laws." A blurry face hovers over your own. "What up queer? Got any last words?"

Your mind struggles to come up with something witty for your final words– something that if said in a movie, would get a chuckle from everyone in the theater. Regrettably, you draw a blank.

Another blast from the shotgun and you expire– your pretty dress completely ruined as your chest opens up for the world to see what you're really made of.

The End

She's gotta just be fuckin' with me, you think to yourself. *I mean, last night was amazing. Why would she all go and leave me like that. It just doesn't make sense. Best to probably just wait here, let her play out her little joke and pretend it's funnier than it really is.* After ten minutes of waiting though, naked, you start to grow restless and feel a little vulnerable.

"Sam? Samantha!" you call out desperately, your voice quickly absorbed by the books all around you. You walk to one of the cross aisles and call again. "Samantha! Hey, are you out there? Ha ha, funny joke. I'm awake now and really would like to put some clothes on," you yell out, turning right then left in the aisle, trying to project your voice farther.

You stop moving for a second and stand very still, straining your ears for any hint of motion or breathing, a sign that would give away her hiding place. You can hear your heart beating in your chest and silence rings in your ears.

"Goddammit, Sam! I'm getting fucking pissed off here. I don't know what kinda fucked up, twisted bitch you are leaving me naked in this goddamn maze, but it's not funny anymore. You need to fucking give me back my clothes!" you scream out angrily, your hands starting to shake you're getting so mad.

You pause again to listen. *Hey, what's that!* You perk up. You can almost make out the sound of snickering coming from somewhere off down one of the aisles.

"I hear you, you fucking bitch. You need to come clean so I can get dressed and get out of here. This isn't as funny as you think it is." You start walking the direction you thought you heard something.

Turn to page 30

Pete said to sit here, so I'm going to sit right here, you tell your sloshed self. You brought him along to keep you from doing anything stupid and he's done pretty well so far. You put your head between your knees and within seconds you pass out.

BEEP, BEEP!! You wake up with a start, your heart beating so hard it feels like it's going to leap from your chest. With your adrenaline racing, you hardly feel drunk anymore and look up to see your car with Pete at the wheel.

"I found it, by God. It was a real bitch since we had parked on the complete opposite side than I thought. Get in!"

You get in the car wordlessly, just wanting to get home and pass out again. Pete tells you that he'll drop you off and then return your car to you tomorrow.

"Sure. Whatever." You fall asleep again quickly, only awakened by Pete's prodding when you're home.

Half-asleep, you make your way up to the front door and drag your drunk ass into the house. You don't quite make it to your room as the couch is looking so incredibly comfortable. You flop down, pull a small throw over mostly your arms and instantly fall asleep. Fitfully, you dream of a clan of semi-naked Klingon women swinging full-sized lumberjack axes at you while you ride away on an ostrich in the rain toward a castle in Romania.

The End

You know you're in trouble. *Time to get the fuck out of here!*

You turn and flee from the antiquated old biddy, turning this way and that, completely losing track of the walls you've followed so carefully, desperate to get away. There is some small part of you that believes that just as enough monkeys in a room can eventually type out Shakespeare's collected works, taking enough turns means you're liable to find the service elevator again and get out of this ninth ring of literary Hell. So far, that glimmer of hope is fading like the tail of a shooting star screaming through the upper reaches of the atmosphere.

Turn right. Right again. Now left. Jesus, this place truly is a endless purgatory of books. **WHAM!** You take a blind corner and slam into a blue uniformed security guard who grasps wildly for the shelf next to him to catch himself.

You're knocked on your ass and slide backwards. The harsh carpet burns your butt cheeks with punishing friction. You scramble to stand back up and flee. The security guard, without missing a beat, lunges at you and knocks you back, twisting your wrists painfully. The two of you struggle. You try in vain to wriggle free from his meaty hands which grab areas no man has ever even been allowed to get close to. You try biting, but the bastard clocks you hard with an elbow to your jaw.

Were this a movie watched in the safety of your living room, you'd no doubt be on the floor laughing at the uncomfortable scene of a naked man writhing around on the floor beneath a hulking, somewhat inept security guard. The inescapable similarity to gay porn would be too much and you'd be choking on popcorn as the gag continued. Unfortunately, being the naked one on the floor with junk flopping dangerously about, throbbing wrists, an indian-burned ass and an animal's desperation for escape– laughter never enters the picture until many years later when you are retelling this story to a friend over cigars and whiskey.

The security guard manages to flip you over onto your stomach and your dick scrapes <u>hard</u> against the sandpapery carpet underneath. He pins your arms and jabs his knee into your back, causing you to yell out in pain. All the commotion brings three other security guards who ziptie your hands and feet. Together they carry you to the service elevator. You are transported to their office where the police pick you up twenty minutes later.

———————————

Turn to page 269

"Hey baby, I came with my homie Thad who's fully hip to your shick friend. How 'bout we leave him his DexterMobile? You gotta cruiser don't ya?"

"Shit yeah, my brother. Drop some bread for our tab and we're Audi 5000." You already paid for your drink at the bar, but you leave a twenty on the table, hoping that'll cover whatever bill is left and follow Foxy who is already sauntering out of the club.

In the parking lot, Foxy walks up to a shiny, black TransAm with a big golden firebird on the hood. You marvel at the horsepower she commands.

"Dy-no-mite! How fast can you get up to in this thing?" you ask as you pull open the door and slide into the bucket seat.

"Fast 'nough to beat any Smokeys on my backdoor," Foxy shoots back at you with a smile.

"Bitchin'!"

Foxy turns the key and the engine roars to life, rumbling with power under the hood. "Hold onto your butt!" Foxy yells as she drops it into gear. Gravel goes flying as the car tears out of the parking lot and onto the street. Gears pop and drop until the car is whistling down the road, easily going forty miles over the speed limit.

"Hey, grab me a Silver Bullet from the backseat?" Foxy asks.

You turn around and see four beers that remain from a six pack of Coors.

"Um...are you sure? I mean, you're driving and everything."

"Don't you worry your pretty little head now. Everybody knows it ain't bootleggin' on this side of the Mississip. Now get me that beer!" You reach in the back and pull off a can. You hand it reluctantly to Foxy who opens it one handed and sucks down a mighty pull. "Besides, I've got my ears on for any County Mounties out and about." Foxy gestures toward a CB radio suspended under the dash.

Despite the breakneck speed and the fact that your driver is drinking, you find yourself intrigued by the CB. You haven't seen one of these in years, and you wonder if anyone else has their "ears on".

Almost in answer to your unspoken question, the CB crackles and a loud voice comes on. "Breaker, breaker. This is King Cobra lookin' for BunnyGirl. You out there BunnyGirl?"

Foxy reaches over and picks up the mic, pushing the talk button. "This is BunnyGirl. Go ahead, over."

"Hey BunnyGirl! Just thought I'd clue you to the brown paper bag that's out on I-40. I just got bit on ma' britches, so back off the hammer if you're headin' that way."

"Roger that King Cobra! Much obliged. Thanks for beating the bushes. I'll catch ya on the flip-flop! 10-4."

You stare at Foxy, flabbergasted. Foxy puts the mic back on the CB and downs the rest of her beer in one gulp, tossing the empty into the backseat.

"What the hell did he say? What's a 'brown paper bag'?"

"An unmarked police car, duh," Foxy responds in a condescending tone. "Also means we'll be takin' the back way home."

After a ridiculous route, you roar up to Foxy's quaint single story ranch. The low slung car scrapes as it enters the driveway. Foxy revs the engine one last time before turning the car off. An eerie silence ensues with the absence of the beastly motor. You can't help but wonder what's in store for you next.

Turn to page 117

You breathe a big sigh, look at Loren and decide you're probably over-reacting. It's not like the two of you had sex or anything. *So what if he likes to dress as a chick? I mean, Lars Olliver in high school used to hit people up with the "Stinkfinger" any chance he could get.* He'd stick his finger in his ass and shove it in your nose. While it sucked, *he* was still your friend; so why can't Loren here dress as a chick?

It's time to grow up, you tell yourself, *and accept that the world is just full of all types of people.* Besides, his driving did save your ass after all.

You pocket your cell and go back to the car. You open the door which is damaged to shit from hitting the other car. You sink back into the passenger seat and stare blankly at the dashboard while you apologize.

"Ok, I'm sorry Loren. I totally freaked out and I'm sorry. You... just... well, you took me by surprise. It was a bit more than I could handle in the moment. The whole having a penis thing... not what I was expecting. I'm sure as hell not gonna kiss you if we get out of this alive, but I think we're cool. K?"

You look at Loren to see how he's accepting your apology and to his credit, he smiles.

"It's ok. I didn't mean to have it happen this way and kinda thrust this on you. I'm glad we're cool. And you really are hot."

"Don't push it, Loren." You smile, knowing that he's right. You add somewhat jokingly, "And please don't EVER use the word 'thrust' with me again."

Turn to page 221

"Sweet dude. I'll take a gin and tonic," you tell him.

Kevin soon returns sporting your drink and a broad smile.

"Let's toast, bro. To a successful night and waking in someone else's bed!"

"No doubt," you agree as you tap your glass to Kevin's. You drink deeply, finishing your drink in a few swallows. The alcohol rapidly absorbs into your bloodstream and you're feeling pretty great.

"Hey, I'm going to hit the dance floor. Wanna come?" you ask Kevin.

"Nah dude, Special K is going to cruise the bar scene first. Don't wanna get all sweaty before it's time," he replies with a wink.

"Suit yourself!" you exclaim and make your way in search of the brunette you saw when you came in.

Once on the dance floor, it's not long before you start feeling the bass of the music rumbling through your body. Your heart seems to adopt the demanding rhythm of the beat, filling you with energy. The heat of the dancing crowd encases you like a warm blanket. You love it.

You dance and dance, grinding up against a number of women who come within your dancing sphere of influence. Every one of them has an electricity about them, sending a glowing, tingling sensation up and down your body. Your senses flare with each touch and you are drawn to them in succession. You bounce up and down, hardly able to separate the concept of yourself from those around you and the mass mentality of the dance floor.

At some point you lose your jacket, but it doesn't matter. Sweat soaks your opened shirt. Your tie flops around in front of you like a fish, slapping your chest in rhythm to your dancing. Every tactile moment is a fantastic rush– every touch of your shirt against your body, the feeling of your pants on your knees, your hair being blown by the enormous fans keeping the air moving. You swear you can even feel the lights streak across your face, burning an array of colors into your vision.

After an exhausting number of songs, you make your way off the dance floor to get some water to satiate your enormous thirst. There is a water fountain by the bathroom, and you attack it with the viciousness of a lion going after its first kill of the day. The cool water drains down your throat and you can feel its glorious fluidity coursing through your whole body. *Oh God, it tastes so good!* You drink and drink, stopping only when you have to breathe.

You rise from the fountain and look around the club. Instantly your head starts to bob again with the house music pulsing through the room. You swear you can feel the walls move and the floor undulate underfoot. *Jesus Christ, I'm so thirsty!* You bend back down and start drinking again. The water is just so cold and tasty and wonderful. You drink in deeply.

"Hey, buddy, mind if I take a turn? You've been there for like fifteen minutes."

You stop drinking to look up and see a line of three or four people waiting for the water fountain. You step aside and let them take drinks in turn, your thirst rising exponentially every minute you have to wait. As the last person in line finishes and turns away, you duck back into the jet of the cool water, letting it play over your tongue, gulping down its sweet reward.

"Hey, are you ok? You've been drinking at that fountain a long ass time."

You stop again, slightly annoyed. "Yeah, I'm fine. I'm just really thirsty. God, I just can't get enough to drink. I think I was dancing too much or something." Your mouth is feeling dry and your thirst climbs dramatically. "Listen, I'm fine, really." You end the conversation and turn back to the fountain to slake your dehydration.

You continue to drink until you are forcefully pulled away from the fountain by a large man dressed in tight fitting polo shirt with the name of the club embroidered on the sleeve. The man adamantly insists that you are coming with him, now. Confused, and still thirsty as hell, you reluctantly go with him.

The two of you step outside and are greeted by an ambulance idling at the curb. You protest that you are totally fine and you were just thirsty, but it falls on deaf ears. The paramedics maintain that you must come with them to be checked out at the hospital. Per policy, you are strapped down for safety sake during the ride. *What fucking overkill*, you think to yourself. During the short ride, your thirst becomes unbearable and you insist on a glass of water or at least a fucking IV. When denied, you start thrashing about on the gurney until finally you are sedated by one of the EMTs.

When you awake a few hours later, a doctor comes to visit you.

"Evening son. To be frank, you're lucky to be alive. You drank enough water tonight that you almost had kidney failure. Seems the ecstasy you took didn't interact well with your body."

"What? Ecstasy? What the hell are you talking about? I didn't take ecstasy! I don't understand. Ecstasy?"

"Yup. The drug disrupted your ability to regulate your water intake and just about killed you."

"I only had one drink and–" you stop. *Holy shit. That bastard Kevin must have slipped it in the gin and tonic he bought me. That fucker!*

"We're going to give you a sedative to help you sleep for another few hours. I'll talk to you more then."

Slipping into unconsciousness, you start planning your revenge on "Special K".

The End

"Ok, ok. You got me on the Portuguese angle. Actually, I thought it would be a great lead in to this cool story about growing up on our family ranch in New Mexico," you lie having really grown up nowhere near there. You develop your lie telling Sofia all about your Spanish best friend and the childhood adventure the two of you had. You claim the two of you singlehandedly stopped a gang of Mexican poachers going after your family's herd of buffalo. You explain how Mexicans eat the gall bladder of buffalos as an aphrodisiac, hoping the bullshit is deep enough she can't paddle out to the other side.

It seems to work. By the end of it, she is spellbound by your manufactured tale of riding and roping, shooting and swearing, saving the buffalo herd from certain slaughter at the hands of the Mexican Gallbladder Reapers. You let out a big sigh internally.

"You have led a very exciting childhood," Sofia exclaims. "I have nothing close to the adventurous tales you tell." She laughs a big laugh, and you are not so sure anymore if she bought your whopper.

"I know, I know," you modestly concede. "It was fun but that's a lifetime away. So, uh, what say we take this conversation elsewhere?"

"Sounds good to me," she replies. "Are you up for another adventure?"

"Sure, what do you have in mind?"

Sofia just winks in answer to your question. "Let's go back to my place. What do you say?"

"I say that is a great idea!" You drop a couple twenties on the bar to pay for your tab, and the two of you leave the bar.

Outside, idling in front, is a huge stretch limo, black as night. A uniformed driver stands beside the limo, and he opens the door upon seeing the two of you.

"Is this for us?" you ask Sofia, incredulously.

"Yes. Shall we get in?" Sofia asks as she glides into the enormous carriage. The driver tips his hat to you as you follow her.

The limousine is cavernous inside. Along one wall, a full wet bar is stocked with top shelf liquors. You hardly have time to take in the opulence before Sofia pulls your head toward hers and the two of you kiss. You've always heard the passion of women south of the equator is legendary. You are drawn to her and the two of you couple effortlessly.

Your blood rages from her kiss and you feel yourself getting extremely aroused. *It's time to bone!* While kissing, you reach up and start to pull down one of the straps of her dress. She breaks away from you.

"Not yet, my American man. There will be plenty of time for that soon. For now, I only desire your lips and your hands. I will welcome the rest of you inside of me when we leave this world far below." She smiles and you can't help but lose yourself in her deep brown eyes and full lips. You fall helplessly back into her embrace and breathe in deep the scent of her hair and skin.

Soon however, the car stops and the door to your right opens. Sofia gets out and you follow behind like a puppy, powerless against her hypnotic sexuality. Suddenly, once out, you realize where you are. You're at the AIRPORT!

"You live at the airport?" you ask, a little dumbstruck by the environment around you. You know it's a stupid question, but your mind is reeling from what's going on. Sofia laughs.

"No, silly. I live in Brasil. I am flying home tonight and you are welcome to come. Would you like to come with me to Brasil?" Sofia looks at you expectantly.

How close am I to my credit card limit?
Hmmm... Fuck it. Let's go!
Turn to page 265

I have to work tomorrow night. I really shouldn't.
Turn to page 157

oft-denied, sad truth of women. You've always had a bit of a problem being THAT guy, but its effectiveness has yet to be challenged. Or, less controversial, it's also widely agreed that chicks can't resist men with foreign accents, and you've perfected a decent British one. While risky, it's at least an avenue that allows you to be less of a jerk.

Take the assertive asshole approach.
Turn to page 106

Be British.
Turn to page 225

You take a long drink of your martini after your toast, imbuing your body with the additional liquid courage necessary for what you feel you need to ask.

"Helen, I don't mean to be a prude here, but are you married?" you ask with trepidation, not sure you really want to hear the answer.

"Way to go, Sherlock. You noticed that, did you?" Helen says with some contempt, taking you back a bit. She holds up her left hand, staring at her wedding ring. After a second, she turns to look at you. "Does that bother you? Fucking a married woman?" she asks.

You stammer for a second, not quite sure what to say. You really want to practice this sexual mythology she commands, but you also don't necessarily want to commit adultery at the same time.

"I can see from the perplexed expression on your face, you don't have an answer just yet. How about I come clean and then you decide?" Helen takes another drink and a deep breath. She turns toward you.

"See, my husband left me four months ago and I confess, I've been very, very lonely ever since." Tears well up in her eyes, and she looks away, clearly ashamed. She blinks her eyes rapidly, holding back the tears, her lips pursed as if she might lose it right in front of you. Humbly, she picks up the bar napkin from underneath her cocktail and dabs the corner of her eyes. She sighs deeply, steadying herself, and then continues, voice subtly shaking. "It was all very sudden. Honestly, I can't even say I saw it coming..." Helen looks down at the bar for a second in reflection before turning back to you, her mood darkened.

"The FUCKTARD ran off with his dental hygienist! He has a dental practice downtown, and one day, the motherfucker just didn't come home. I guess teeth weren't the only thing he was drilling at work, huh? So, long story short, I'm pretty sure he ran off with her to Arizona, judging from our credit card statements. What an asshole!" Helen is clearly filled with rage, her hands clenched. The sadness in her voice has turned angry with a tinge of pure hate.

She looks at you with her frustrated, wet, puppy dog eyes. "So that's my story, take it or leave it."

Dammit! you swear to yourself. *Why the hell did I bring it up?!* You feel bad for making Helen relate her painful story. You also feel kinda bad for yourself. This sure isn't the way you wanted the night to end– listening to some sad sob story told by this old mare.

"I'm really sorry," you apologize. "I shouldn't have pried. That's a horrible tale. What a real douche that guy is!"

Helen smiles an acceptance to your apology. She then asks in a quiet voice, "So what do you say, champ? Still willing to have a little adventure with an older woman who's got plenty of money and a desire to fuck the shit out of anyone she meets?"

Fuck, this decision hasn't gotten any easier! Now, the question that begs to be answered is: Would fucking Helen be taking advantage of her in her broken state, or is it ok since it's clearly something she wants and might actually be therapeutic for her!

———————————

Let her down easy and say goodbye.
Turn to page 230

Mercy fuck her.
Turn to page 231

"Not fer nothin' but moight I be enquirin' a wee bit mohr about yer tattoo? I git tha sense dat ya got a moighty intarestin' story thar and I'd be lovin' ta hear it!"

"What the fuck!" Dixie sighs. "Why the fuck do you have to keep bringing up my tat? Ok Frenchy, here's the deal. If you wanna hear about my tattoo, you're gonna have to fuck it out of me," Dixie replies drunkenly, slurring her words. "That's the only way I'm gonna tell you about prison."

Whoa. What did she just say?

"Did ya say 'prison' jus than? Was I hearin' ya roight?" you ask.

"BBBBBBSssssshhaw. What? No. I didn't say nothing about prison. Oh for Christ's sake, do you wanna fuck or what, ya English fag?"

Hmmmm… she's really piqued your interest now. *What the hell could this gorgeous woman have gone to prison for?!* You rack your brain trying to come up with scenarios. *I mean, she's incredibly well dressed and aside from being a bit of a hostile and aggressive drunk now, she's been quite the lady most of the night.*

Or, it could all be an act? She could be one of those Black Widows who lure men back to their place and then rob and kill them. God, maybe she really meant to mention prison. Dammit! You're really unsure if you should take the chance of going home with her. Although, are you being a pussy if you don't?

Go with her.
Turn to page 327

Your vagina hurts too much.
Turn to page 228

"Fuck you, bitch! I'm not paying for shit! How dare you fuckin' bring me to this shithole and then presume I'm going to pay for sex with you! Fuck you, cunt!"

Maggie stands up angrily, while you struggle to get your underwear and pants pulled up over your mighty warrior. "Fuck me? Fuck you muthafucka!" Maggie's voice suddenly changes dialect from Irish to Jersey native. "Jonesy! Get the fuck in 'ere! We gots us a John that thinks he's too fuckin' gud to pay."

The door of the back bedroom opens. Out comes one of the most massive black men you have ever seen. You know you're in deep shit as he comes striding determinedly toward you, a scowl on his face. Maggie backs out of his way, making you even more nervous.

"Toss this shithead out and don't be nice about et!" Maggie commands.

"Wait a second. Wait a second," you say hurriedly. "I mean, there's no reason to all get mad here. Listen Maggie, if that's your real name, I'm sorry. I'm REALLY sorry. I didn't mean what I said. I know, how about I give you a hundred bucks and I just leave peacefully? How 'bout that?" You go for your wallet and pull out a few twenties, not counting it, hoping it's at least a hundred dollars.

"Wait a sec, Jonesy. Let's see what Jackass here is offerin'." Maggie reaches out and snatches the money from you. She counts it. "I dunno, bub. This is $140. I mean, that's enough for me, but what about Jonesy 'ere? You all woke the man up, and he don't like bein' woken up."

You open your wallet again to find a single twenty, a few ones and a five.

"I've got like $27 left. Is that enough? Here, it's all yours." You hand the money with a shaking hand to Maggie.

"That's it? That's all? Eh, fuck 'em up Jonesy. See ya later, bub!"

Jonesy steps in and grabs you roughly by the collar of your suit jacket. With massive force, he tosses you down the hallway toward the apartment's exit. Your face smashes into the solid metal door, the small brass ring around the peephole burying itself into your forehead. You fall back but are caught by Jonesy.

He grabs you again with one hand, using the other to open the door. He then drags you out in the hallway and launches you down the stairs. You make a futile attempt to grab the railing but it doesn't help. You tumble down the stairs hurdling into the landing's wall with your shoulder. You feel your collarbone snap painfully. You muster your strength and stand up as quick as you can. With the worst pain staved off by adrenaline, you descend the rest of the stairs ahead of Jonesy who is striding behind you, taking the stairs at a slower, determined pace.

At the bottom of the stairs, you fling open both doors and dart into the night, the dingy street much preferred to the hell that is following you. Once outside you look back to see the large man standing behind the inner door, not willing to follow you out. He crosses his arms, making it known that to reenter is certain pain.

You turn back toward the street and shoot your hand into your pocket for your car keys. You start to pull them out when you notice that your car is missing. In its place, behind Maggie's early 90's Ford, is a glaring gap. The long, barren curb stares at you as if your car had never existed.

"Shit!" you scream angrily, cursing the universe for tonight. "Goddammit!"

You walk over to where your car used to be and amble around in its spot, desperately wishing that maybe it's just invisible or will reappear. No luck.

While casting about for your lost car, a rumble breaks the silence of the night as a city bus turns the corner two blocks down. Unwilling to wait any longer in this rundown assturd of a neighborhood, you flag down the bus as it approaches.

The door opens and you get on, searching in your pockets for any change you may have left after being robbed by that slut whore fucknugget. You manage to produce forty-one cents. With a pained look, you hand it to the bus driver. He shakes his head slowly at you, as if to say: *You poor, poor dumb schmuck. Something horrible must have obviously happened to you to be dressed all nice in this asswhiff side of town.* The driver motions for you to move on to the bus and closes the door. You sink down in a seat, exhaling a big sigh, glad that the night is <u>finally</u> over.

On your extended bus ride home, you share the bus with a number of denizens of the early predawn hours. Nearby a woman with crazy, mousey, grey hair snores raucously. A few seats away from her, two old men argue loudly, albeit mostly incoherently. After a few miles you realize that they are both arguing with imaginary passengers rather than with each other. You shake your head in disbelief that this is your life right now.

To top off your night though, three stops before you are to disembark, a man wearing a long, gray, stained raincoat walks by on his way to the rear exit of the bus. He flashes you. Completely taken off guard, you inadvertently stare right at him. To your horror, his skinny, pale body highlights at his waist an unfortunate rendition of a sticky piece of white taffy dropped on the floor of an African American barbershop. You hate your life.

The End

You stride over to the honeys, clearly directing your attention to the woman in pink.

"Peep this bootylicious brick house," you announce to the surrounding club. "Don't break foul on this cat, but you musta laid down some cheese on them there threads. Smokin'!"

Glowing pink in the ambient light, the Spandex Goddess answers your 70's cat call with a smile. Following your ostentatious lead, Thad leans in and introduces himself to her compatriot in a more subdued fashion. The two of them strike up a conversation and leave for the dance floor in no time. *God, I love Thad,* you say to yourself. *Helluva wingman!*

"Name's Foxy. Foxy Cleopatra Jones. You're a bit of stone fox yourself. Mmmm." Foxy gives you a sly, sexy glance. *Oh hell yeah, she's deep into this 70's shit,* you think.

"What can I say, I'm just keepin' it real, baby. And listin' here, before you start thinkin' otherwise, I gotta tell ya I'm no operator, can ya dig it? One woman only, and I think that cat should be you." Just then, you hear a new song come on, one that can take advantage of your singular line dancing talents. If you're going to have to dance tonight, this would be the best time.

You hit up Foxy, "What say you and I get our groove on?"

"Righteousness. Enough confabin' for me. Let's boogie!"

You take Foxy's hand and make your way to the pulsating dance floor. The dancing crowd undulates back and forth doing the LA Bus Stop Hustle. The two of you enthusiastically join in– stepping, crossing and hopping to the music. You're in the zone and not even Travolta could outshine you now. You have a great time bustin' it with Foxy, occasionally givin' her a wink now and again.

After the doing the Hustle, you quickly exaggerate your tiredness and need for beer to escape the next song. Foxy begrudgingly follows you, all the while funkin' to the music on the way to the table. Safe again from the potential mixed-use, two story building. She has numerous big picture windows on one wall that overlook the quiet, tree-lined street and a bakery below. Through the floorboards, you can smell the fresh bread and rolls already baking for the breakfast crowd arriving a few hours from now. *What a great place to live!*

Once inside, the two of you tumble onto the couch by the enormous windows. You kick off your shoes and throw your suit coat to the floor. The two of you kiss passionately, the alcohol driving both of you into a hormonal frenzy. Loud and obnoxiously, your lips meet first on her mouth, then play down her neck to the exposed flesh within the deep V-cut of her dress. You toss her onto her back, and she extends her slender figure along the couch. You lean over her and run one hand up her exposed leg, jutting sensuously from the extended slit up her dress. Your hand travels slowly, starting above her knee, taking in the warm, supple, soft nature of her skin. You move up further, beneath her dress, up to her hip. Not a shred of underwear disrupts the flow of her body underhand. This simple fact makes you involuntarily pulse with anticipation.

In response, Dixie reaches up and pushes you roughly with both hands, sex burning in her eyes. You fall back slightly to a seated position, your arm along the top of the couch. Her hands, still on your shirt, stroke lightly down your chest before grabbing opposing sides and jerking your shirt open. Buttons rain down on the floor like a miniature hail storm, clattering and rolling around. Her hands then move south to your pants, fumbling but ultimately succeeding in unbuttoning your belt, pulling it out with a audible *crack*. The belt follows the buttons to the floor. Dixie then unbuttons your pants and reaches one hand in, slowly working her way down your cock. You lean back, eyes closed and groan low with an outpouring of sexual desire.

Dixie smiles at you and strokes you slowly a few times before leisurely withdrawing her hand, causing you to vibrate with ecstasy. She works her fingers up your stomach to your chest and then grabs your tie, jerking you down atop her, pulling your head to her shoulder. Her lips find your ear, and her teeth nibble nimbly on it. She whispers ever so quietly over the pounding blood whooshing in your ear, "Do you really want to hear about my tattoo?"

Fuck that. Let's fuck!
Turn to page 71

Yes, but make it quick.
Turn to page 196

You stand up, a little wobbly, and start weaving your way toward the bazillions of cars ahead. In the dim parking lot lights it's hard to make out the color of any car; and given the creativity of automakers today, the shapes of all of them largely look identical.

You wander aimlessly like a Christmas shopper in the mall's parking lot, casting about for any semblance of a car that looks familiar. *Goddammit, why couldn't I be one of those fuckin' hippie pinko leftists that cover the back of their car with random propaganda.* It'd be super easy to find your car then! Argh!

Around and around you walk, getting frustrated. You begin to get maudlin about the whole situation. *God, if I just hadn't drank so much, I'd remember where the car is.*

"FUCK!" you cry out to empty ears, not believing how screwed you are. It was those stupid sci-fi chicks! If they hadn't pretended that they were foreign and had you keep drinking, believing that you were going to get lucky, none of this would have happened. *Moreover, why the hell did Pete let this go on for so long? I mean, for Chrissake, you invited him along for this very reason! He was supposed to make sure that you didn't get too drunk and do something stupid.*

Well fuck! Look at me now, you think. *I'm lost in this friggin' used car lot, blasted out of my mind, and I'm never going to get home. Never! Oh God, this sucks.*

You find yourself starting to whimper uncontrollably, feeling infinitely sorry for yourself, blaming just about everyone for your current predicament. Giving up, you hunker down between two parked cars. You cup your knees to your chest and begin to cry. It doesn't last too long though as the alcohol causes you to quickly pass out. (It's probably for the best, you're being a real pussy.)

When you awaken, the first rays of light are coming over the horizon and morning is upon you. You feel a little cold. You sit up, having fallen over and sprawled out while you were asleep. In doing so, you notice that you are no longer wearing your pants and shoes! Your ridiculous bikini underwear does little to help against the cold of the breaking dawn. You stand up and put your hands into your jacket pockets to try to conserve some body heat.

Inside your pocket you feel a piece of torn paper. You pull it out to find a little note scribbled on it:

Hey Bud,

> *Thanks for the pants and shoes! Mine were getting so bad I finally had to throw them out. Hope the hangover isn't too horrible. Karma will surely pay ya back.*

> *Cheers,*
> *Mike the Bum*

"Fuuuuuuuuuck!" you scream at the top of your lungs. Moreover, you discover that not only do you not have your pants and shoes, Mike took your wallet and phone. *Shit!* Even if you borrow a phone, being a product of modern society, you don't remember anyone's number– why would you, it's all in your GODDAMN cell! You sigh. It's going to be a long day.

The End

dance. "So like she was all up on my junk and shit, fuckin' so much so that I thought I might bust a nut in my pants. She was all petting me and stroking my shit. It was fuckin' amazing, bro! Then she all started stickin' her ass in my face, so I said what the hell and stuck a finger in. She got all pissed and shit, but then reconsidered and said she'll give me a hand job for fifty bucks. Dude, you've <u>totally</u> gotta sport me some cash. I'm all tapped out and that bitch was smokin'."

Rather drunk, you reach for your wallet and sport Kevin fifty dollars.

"Thanks dude. I totally owe you one." Spurred on by Kevin's success story, you decide a lap dance is not a bad idea. After the dancer at your stage is finished, you get up from your chair and meet her coming down from the stage. Being a pro, the stripper dispenses with any question of small talk.

"Hey there big spender, want to take the next dance in the back?" she asks with a smile.

Not to be outdone by Kevin, you decide to up the ante a little. "Sure but listen, as hot as you are, I think you should bring a friend." The stripper just smiles and tells you to wait a sec. In a few moments she returns with a stunning brunette on her arm. The brunette is clad only in a white, oversized, man's dress shirt and a baseball cap– her ponytail sticking out the back. *Oh, fuck yeah!*

The three of you go to a back room and to the tune of a c-note, you get three songs of glorious fondling, the girls touching you everywhere– nothing's off limits. In fact, at the climax of one song, the brunette even sticks her hand down your pants and strokes you off a little. It's the shit, although nothing compares to the final song's girl on girl action that you have an exclusive seat for. *Sweet Jesus it's erotic!*

After it's over you untuck your shirt and pull it down over the front of your trousers. You're barely able to walk without showing off how great the private dance was. Solo now, you make you way back to the club proper and find Kevin. It turns out "the cunt wasn't interested anymore" so

Kevin blew the fifty dollars on a few consolation shots. You relate your dance to Kevin, and instantly he's back in the game. The two of you head to the red stage and you begrudgingly sport Kevin some more cash.

Over the next hour, it's a blur of women and booze, your wallet pouring out ones and fives. Nothing breaks the stride of the night until Bambi takes the stage. Not the best looking of the bunch, Bambi goes right to action, disrobing immediately and prancing around the platform. Her routine is largely typical of what you've already seen and doesn't inspire much until her third and final song. It's a sultry disco number that you know you've heard before, but the haze of booze is too much for your gray matter to extract the title right now.

Ever the professional, Bambi makes her way to you and Kevin, seeking a bill to dance for. Unbeknownst to her, at this point during the night you only have a twenty dollar bill left and you'll be damned if you're going to give it to this chick. Bambi however, knows her craft and lowers her big doe eyes squarely at you. She bends down slowly before you and leans in between you and Kevin.

"How about a trick, fellas?"

"Sure, baby. What you got that I haven't seen before?" Kevin responds, his dick doing most of the talking.

"Let's just say I'll blow your mind."

Ok, heard it, you think to yourself. You've had the ultimate lap dance, you're drunker than shit– what could this chick possibly have to offer that the night has yet to provide?

"Sorry, honey," you say, "but I'm down to my last twenty and I can't say I'm feeling it."

"How 'bout this, sugar? You put your twenty on the stage, and if I don't wow you, you get it back as well as a free lap dance for the both of you."

"He'll do it!" Kevin chimes in for you. "Dude, give her the bill. I gotta see this."

You look over at Kevin, his face ruddy from the alcohol, his eyes starting to droop. "I don't know, Kev. I've dropped almost three hundred bucks and it's–"

With a speed you didn't expect from someone as drunk as your friend, Kevin grabs your wallet from your hands and pulls out the twenty. He throws it onstage.

With a flourish and a smile, Bambi quickly grabs the twenty, creases it in half lengthwise and places it gingerly over the bottom of her underwear. She then looks at you, smiles, and *POOF!* the bill flies off and sails a good foot or two across the stage.

"Holy SHIT! That chick just pussyfarted your twenty like a good three feet! That was fuckin' amazing!" Kevin yells. You admit to yourself that it's quite the talent and you're more than happy at this point to NOT get the twenty back. "Dude, did you see it?!" Kevin frantically asks.

"Yeah, I saw it," you respond, impressed but not sure it was worth twenty bucks.

Not to be outdone, Kevin addresses the stripper who is finished with her three songs and collecting money off the stage. "Hey baby, I'll give you that that was impressive. But, what do you think about this?!" Kevin grabs the front of his shirt and true to form, rips it open, buttons flying everywhere.

Here we go again, you think.

"Ever seen a chest like this honey? I work out every day."

"Nice," Bambi responds, obviously unimpressed and cognoscente of the fact that Kevin has no more money.

"Nice? Shit bitch, this body is the bomb! I'm a fucking temple. I know you whores can't resist a cut like this. What say you and I go have some fun?"

"How about another time, friend." Bambi is clearly getting a little nervous with Kevin's overbearing ego and proposition.

"How about now, cunt?!"

"Okay buddy, that's enough out of you." A brusque, burly member of house security steps into the exchange. The two of them go head to head, Kevin insisting on showing off his toned body in a sad attempt to intimidate the bouncer. In the end, Kevin is ejected from the club, and the cops are called. He's arrested and you have to call a cab being way too drunk to drive home.

You realize, in retrospect, three hundred dollars poorer and sleeping alone for another night– Kevin was a bad choice in wingmen.

The End

You decide not to stop. Sure you could try pretending to be a car in someone's driveway, but if you were spotted… that'd probably be the end of you. Best to keep on going.

You coach Loretta through the streets, burying yourself and your pursuers deeper and deeper into the neighborhood. Finally after an hour, you use a roundabout to circle back behind the pickups and slowly make your way toward the exit. About a mile before you depart Classical Estates, you turn around and watch anxiously if you are being followed anymore. Na'er a single headlight comes into view. You start getting butterflies in your stomach.

At the exit, you ask Loretta to pull over for a second. Loretta parks in front of the huge illuminated wooden sign for the neighborhood. Heart beating fast and elated beyond words, you turn to Loretta and announce excitedly, "We did it! We fuckin' did it!"

Being free takes a second to sink in for Loretta. As it does, you can visibly see the stress lift from her– her body sinking down into the seat, a wash of relief coming across her face.

"We did, didn't we. Oh my God, I was so scared! I really didn't think we could get away. I've never been in a situation like that before."

"You did great, Loretta. The way you drove, how you kept a level head– I'm totally impressed. God, I think I could kiss you." Which, you decide, is exactly what you want to do. You unbuckle your seatbelt, take Loretta's face with both hands and go in for a long celebratory kiss. After it is over, you know you want this woman more than you've ever wanted someone before. She's gorgeous and brave and man, can she handle a car!

"How about we…uh… head back to your place and relax after all this excitement. Would that be cool?" you ask.

In response, Loretta just smiles at you and pulls away from the curb. It's not long before the two of you are in her apartment, lusting hungrily after one another. It's a wonderful night, both of you channeling your excitement of the chase into powerful love making. You do things that you've dreamed about doing with a woman, but no woman ever acquiesced. It's a night like none other. After hours of making love, you fall fast asleep, exhausted on every level.

The next morning, you awaken slowly. Rays of sunlight creep in through the window bringing you out of your slumber naturally. You place your hands behind your head and think back to the adventures of the night before– the bar fight, the chase, the incredible sex. You breathe in deeply and notice the wonderful odor of bacon and eggs and coffee. *God, now there's a woman! You gotta love someone who will service you at night, and then again in the morning with breakfast.*

You languidly roll out of bed and decide you're going to surprise Loretta with a full show for breakfast. You forsake any clothes littered on the floor and make your way down the hallway to the kitchen. The sound of frying bacon grows louder and the smell, ahhh the smell is to die for. You find your mouth watering, both for the awaiting breakfast and another kiss from this amazing woman.

"Good morning, honey!" you announce as you round the corner.

Unexpectedly, you find a short man standing in front of the stove, spatula in hand. He has close-cropped, brown hair and is wearing an ornate Chinese kimono, smoking a cigarette. He turns around, seeing you completely naked and smiles.

"Good morning, dear! Eggs?"

The End

"Sure. That's fine by me. But listen, I've had quite the night already, and all I want to do at this point is get home. Are you cool with dropping me off first?"

"Oh yeah. No problem at all," she responds.

"Then my cab is your cab. Please, after you." The woman gets in and you follow her. The taxi rapidly pulls away from the curb and makes for the exit of the airport complex. You lean forward to the Plexiglas window that separates passengers from the driver to let him know your address.

You sit back and further examine the woman beside you. Her coat has opened a bit more at the top so you can now see she's wearing a fashionable black dress with ringed in lace covering a very nice set of hooters.

"So, what's your name?" you ask.

"Margaret," she responds succinctly.

"What brings you to this neck of the woods?"

"Work," Margaret answers. She smiles at you and then looks out the rear window of the taxi. After a few moments, she turns to look out her own window. *Hmmm, not very talkative.* You let the pseudo-conversation drop and ride for a little while in silence. Unfortunately for Margaret, in your drunken state you tend to be a bit loquacious and silence is just not something you can deal with for very long.

"So, what do you think about this weather we're having? Oh that's right, my bad. You just got in. Stupid me." You laugh. "So like we've been having this really annoying weather recently!" You continue to prattle on about the weather with no real concern if Margaret is paying attention or not. After randomly babbling on about the weather for a while, you switch subjects to football, then basketball, then your guinea pig "Squeakers" you had growing up, then your love for pasta. It's more or less a stream of consciousness that's coming out of your mouth. You're largely talking just to hear yourself talk.

"I'm sorry but did you say that you had a guinea pig?" Margaret suddenly interjects.

"Why yes I did!" you respond happily. "His name was Squeakers and he had this great maze that I built for him. It was really cool with all these twists and turns. I made the whole thing from PVC pipe. How about you? Do you have a guinea pig?" you ask.

"What? Uh... no. So, where's a great place to get a burger around here?"

"Well... there's Gordy's over off of First Street but they're a little greasy for my taste. You could also try McShale's. They have this great buffalo burger with guac and salsa that's to die for. Do you like guac? I love guac. Some people say it's slimy, but not me. I love the stuff."

"Uh huh," Margaret responds absentmindedly, looking out the rear window of the taxi again. She turns. "Didn't you say you like sports?"

"Hell yeah!" you respond. She must have missed the ten minutes you just spent talking all about football and basketball. You start again to tell her all about your favorite team. After a few minutes, you notice that she isn't listening and is staring out the back window of the cab.

"What are you looking for?" you ask.

"What? Oh nothing. It's nothing. I uh... I just like looking at the stars and you know, you just can't see them very well from the side windows."

"Gotcha. You're totally right," you say. "So, whereabouts did you grow up?"

"Can I ask you something?" she responds. "If I wanted to stay here for a few days, what hotel would you recommend?" Margaret's big brown eyes look at you inquisitively.

"Well, there's a Marriot downtown that's pretty cool. Or if you need something a bit more budget-friendly, you could always try out the Stinson Suites off Indiana Avenue."

"Ok. Ok. Indiana Avenue. Sounds good." Margaret turns away from you and stares out her window at the snaking yellow line on the pavement beside the taxi. She then cocks her head to look up at the stars. After a cursory study of the sky, she turns toward you to smile briefly before looking out the back of the cab again. You turn in your seat and look back at the road trailing behind. You realize that Margaret didn't have any luggage. *Hmmm, that's kinda strange.* You look over at her.

"Did you at least have a nice flight here?"

"Oh yes, it was very nice," she responds and then turns to look out her window again. *Damn, she's a odd duck. Oh well. No worries. I'll be home soon and she can just go on being weird.*

The taxi saunters up to the curb and parks with the engine idling. You reach into your pocket, pull out some cash and hand it to the driver.

"Have a nice night, Margaret, wherever you end up," you toss off casually as you open your door.

"Hey, I was doing some thinking and wanted to see if I might join you for a drink inside?" Margaret asks in a sudden friendly tone that takes you off guard.

"Oh, I dunno," you respond cautiously. "I'm really tired and I've got work tomorrow and well... that's about the size of it. Tired, sleepy, wanna go to bed."

"Oh come on. Just one little drinkypoo. I've been flying all day and then I meet you and hear all about Squeakers and your love for pasta and I think to myself: 'Self, this guy is all right. You should have a drink with him.' So, what do ya say?" Margaret looks at you expectantly with pouty lips and big doe eyes.

She a bit of freak show. Tell her 'No.'
Turn to page 158

Oh, what could it hurt. Invite her in.
Turn to page 160

9645069R0020

Made in the USA
Charleston, SC
29 September 2011